D1385481

**Anger settled between his brows. 'I want to just enjoy today. Enjoy your company. Like we used to.'**

And he didn't want it to stop, which was not what she'd expected when she got out of the taxi sixty floors below. She thought he'd have just shrugged and wished her well and found someone else to start an annual Christmas tradition with.

'Well, things have changed now,' she urged. 'Like it or not.'

Something flickered in his eyes, his face grew unnaturally intent. And she grew inexplicably nervous.

'So,' he started, 'if we're not friends what are we?'

She choked slightly on her wine. 'Sorry?'

'I accept that we're not friends. But I wonder, then, what that means we are.'

She just stared.

'Because there were two things that defined our relationship for me...' He used the word "defined" as though it meant "constrained". 'One was that you were the wife of a friend. Now—tragically—no longer the case. And the other was that we were friends. Apparently also now no longer the case. So, tell me, Audrey—'

He leaned forward and swilled the liquid in his glass and his eyes locked on hard to hers.

'—where exactly does that leave us?'

Dear Reader,

Have you ever heard the saying, 'Why let the truth get in the way of a perfectly good story'? A friend told me how she catches up, once a year, with a longstanding (male) friend in a gorgeous restaurant high above a beautiful Asian city. They spend a full, lazy day catching up and sharing stories and squeezing a year's worth of friendship into that one day of the year and then they fly back to their respective countries. And it's entirely, completely, unquestionably wholesome.

So of course I had to go and ruin it.

The simple premise grabbed me and filled me to overflowing with those 'what ifs' that authors love. What if it wasn't completely wholesome? What if one of them was secretly attracted to the other one but never, ever planned to act on it? What if they did this for years and then one year *something changed…*?

And I realized that this story was really about the biggest 'what if' of all…one that we can all relate to. What if you'd turned right instead of left that day, or taken the bus instead of walking, or been brave enough to give your phone number to one man instead of his friend? What if you'd just grabbed opportunity by the shirt-collar the first time around? Where would you be today?

This is a story about the patience of Love, the beauty of Friendship and the magic of Christmas.

If you're reading it at Christmas, please accept my best wishes to you and your family for a wonderful and safe holiday season.

May love always find you,

*Nikki*

www.nikkilogan.com.au – A Romance with Nature

# HIS UNTIL MIDNIGHT

BY
NIKKI LOGAN

First published in Great Britain 2013
by Mills & Boon, an imprint of Harlequin (UK) Limited,
Harlequin (UK) Limited, Eton House, 18-24 Paradise Road,
Richmond, Surrey TW9 1SR

© Nikki Logan 2013

ISBN: 978 0 263 23585 2

Harlequin (UK) policy is to use papers that are natural, renewable and recyclable products and made from wood grown in sustainable forests. The logging and manufacturing processes conform to the legal environmental regulations of the country of origin.

Printed and bound in Great Britain
by CPI Antony Rowe, Chippenham, Wiltshire

**Nikki Logan** lives next to a string of protected wetlands in Western Australia, with her long-suffering partner and a menagerie of furred, feathered and scaly mates. She studied film and theatre at university, and worked for years in advertising and film distribution before finally settling down in the wildlife industry. Her romance with nature goes way back, and she considers her life charmed, given she works with wildlife by day and writes fiction by night—the perfect way to combine her two loves. Nikki believes that the passion and risk of falling in love are perfectly mirrored in the danger and beauty of wild places. Every romance she writes contains an element of nature, and if readers catch a waft of rich earth or the spray of wild ocean between the pages she knows her job is done.

For Alex and Trev who let me turn their entirely platonic annual tradition into something much more dramatic. Thank you for the inspiration.

# CHAPTER ONE

*December 20th, four years ago*
*Qīngtíng Restaurant, Hong Kong*

AUDREY DEVANEY FLOPPED against the back of the curved sofa and studied the pretty, oriental-style cards in her hands. Not the best hand in the world but when you were playing for M&M's and you tended to eat your stake as fast as it accumulated it was hard to take poker too seriously.

Though it was fun to pretend she knew what she was doing. Like some Vegas hotshot. And it wasn't too hard to imagine that the extraordinary view of Hong Kong's Victoria Harbour stretching out behind Oliver Harmer was really out of the window of some casino high-roller's room instead of a darkened, atmospheric restaurant festooned with pretty lanterns and baubles in rich, oriental colours.

Across from her, Oliver's five o'clock shadow was designer perfect and an ever-present, unlit cigar poked out of the corner of his grinning mouth—more gummed than smoked, out of respect for her and for the other patrons in the restaurant. It only *felt* as if he bought the whole place out each Christmas, it wasn't actually true. Though it was nice to imagine that they had the entire restaurant to themselves.

'Thank you, again, for the gift,' she murmured, letting the fringed silk ends of the cobalt scarf run between her fingers. 'It's stunning.'

'You're welcome. You should wear more blue.'

Audrey studied Oliver over her cards, wanting to ask but not entirely sure how to raise it. Maybe the best approach was the direct approach...

'You know, you look pretty good for a man whose wedding just fell through.'

'Good' as in *well*. Not 'good' as in *gorgeous*. Although, as always, the latter would certainly apply. All that dark hair, long lashes and tanned Australian skin...

He took his time considering his hand and then tossed three cards face down onto the ornate carved table. 'Dodged a bullet.'

That stopped her just as she might have discarded her own dud cards. 'Really? Last Christmas it was all about how Tiffany might be "the one".'

Not that she'd actually believed him at the time, but a year was the longest relationship she'd ever known him to have.

Maybe she was just in denial.

'Turns out there was more than one "one" for Tiffany.' The tiniest glimmer of hurt stained his eyes.

Oh, no. 'Who called it off?'

His answer came fast and sure. 'I did.'

Oliver Harmer was a perpetual bachelor. But he was also Shanghai's most prized perpetual bachelor and so she couldn't imagine the average woman he dated being too fast to throw away her luxury future.

But she knew from Blake how seriously Oliver felt about fidelity. Because of his philandering father. 'I'm so sorry.'

He shrugged. 'She was with someone when I met her; I was foolish to think that I'd get treated any different.'

Foolish perhaps, but he was only human to hope that he'd be special enough to change his girlfriend's ways. And if ever there was a man worth changing for... Audrey dropped two cards onto the table and Oliver flicked her two replacements from the top of the pack with confident efficiency before taking three of his own.

'What did she say when you confronted her?' she murmured.

'I didn't see any purpose in having it out,' he squeezed out past the cigar. 'I just cut her loose.'

Without an explanation? 'What if you were mistaken?'

The look he threw her would have withered his corporate opponents. 'I checked. I wasn't.'

'Checking' in Oliver's world probably meant expensive private surveillance. So no, he wouldn't have been wrong. 'Where is she now?'

He shrugged. 'Still on our honeymoon, I guess. I gave her an open credit card and wished her the best.'

'You bought her off?' She gaped.

'I bought her forgiveness.'

'And that worked?'

'Tiffany never was one for labouring under regret for long.'

Lord, he had a talent for ferreting out the worst of women. Always beautiful, of course and—*cough*— agile, but utterly barren on the emotional front. To the point that she'd decided Oliver must prefer them that way. Except for the trace of genuine hurt that had flitted across his expression…

That didn't fit with the man she thought she knew.

She studied the nothing hand in front of her and then tossed all five cards down on the table in an inelegant fold.

'Why can't you just meet a nice, normal woman?' she despaired. 'Shanghai's a big city.'

He scooped the pile of bright M&M's towards him— though not before she snaffled yet another one to eat—and set about reshuffling the cards. 'Nice women tend to give me a wide berth. I can't explain it.'

She snorted. 'It would have nothing to do with your reputation.'

Hazel eyes locked on hers, speculative and challenging. Enough to tighten her chest a hint. 'And what reputation is that?'

*Ah...no.* 'I'm not going to feed your already massive ego, Oliver.'

Nor go anywhere near the female whispers she'd heard about Oliver *'the Hammer'* Harmer. Dangerous territory.

'I thought we were friends!' he protested.

'You're friends with my husband. I'm just his South-East Asian proxy.'

He grunted. 'You only agree to our ritual Christmas catch-up for the cuisine, I suppose?'

'Actually, no.'

She found his eyes—held them—and two tiny butterflies broke free in her chest. 'I come for the wine, too.'

He snagged a small fistful of M&M's and tossed them across the elegant, carved coffee table at her, heedless of those around them sharing the Christmas-themed menu sixty storeys above Hong Kong.

Audrey scrabbled madly to pick them up. 'Ugh. Isn't that just like a squazillionaire. Throwing your money around like it's chocolate drops.'

'Play your hand,' he griped. But there was a definite smile behind it. As there always was. Christmases between them were always full of humour, fast conversation and camaraderie.

At least on the surface.

Below the surface was a whole bunch of things that she didn't let herself look at too closely. Appreciation. Respect. A great, aching admiration for his life and the choices he'd made and the courage with which he'd made them. Oliver Harmer was the freest human being she knew. And he lived a life most people would hunger for.

She certainly did from within the boundaries of her awkward marriage. It was hard not to esteem his choices.

And then below all of that… The ever-simmering attraction. She'd grown used to it now, because it was always there. And because she only had to deal with it once a year.

He was a good-looking man; charming and affable, easy to talk to, easy to like, well built, well groomed, well mannered, but not up himself or pretentious. Never too cool to toss a handful of chocolates in a fine restaurant.

But he'd also been best man at her wedding.

Blake's oldest friend.

And he was pursued by women day in and day out. She would be two hundred per cent mortified if Oliver ever got so much of a hint of the direction of her runaway thoughts—not the least because it would just inflate his already monumental ego—but also because she knew exactly what he'd do with the information.

*Nothing.*

Not a damned thing.

He would take it to his grave, and she would never fully know if that was because of his loyalty to Blake, his respect for her, or because something brewing between them was just so totally inconceivable that he'd chalk it up to an aberrant moment best never again spoken of.

Which was pretty much the right advice.

She wasn't like the women he normally chose. Her finest day was the day of her wedding when she'd been called 'striking'—and by Oliver, come to think of it, who always seemed to say the right thing at the right moment when she was on rocky emotional ground. She didn't look as good as his women did in their finery and she didn't move in the same circles and know the same people and laugh overly loud at the same stories. She wasn't unattractive or dull or dim—she'd wager the entire pile of M&M's in front of her on the fact that she could outrank every one of them on a

MENSA test—but she certainly didn't turn heads when she was in the company of the beautiful people. She lacked that…stardust that they had.

That Oliver was coated-to-sparkling in.

And in all the years she'd known him, she'd flat out never seen him with someone less beautiful than he was.

Clearly some scientific principle of balance at work there.

And when even the laws of nature ruled you out…

'All right, Cool Hand Luke,' she said, ripping her thoughts back to safer territory. 'Let's get serious about this game.'

That treacherous snake.

Audrey clearly had no idea whatsoever of Blake's latest conquest. Her face had filled just then with genuine sympathy about Tiffany, but nothing else. No shadows of pain at the mention of someone's infidelity, no blanching. No tears for a betrayal shared. Not that she was the tears-in-public type, but the only moisture in those enormous blue eyes was old-fashioned compassion.

For him.

Which meant that either Blake had lied and Audrey had no idea that her husband considered their marriage open, or she *did* know and Blake had worn her down to the point that she just didn't care any more.

And that awful possibility just didn't fit with the engaged, involved woman in front of him.

Oliver eyed her over his cards, pretending to psych her out and throw her game but really using the opportunity to study the tiniest traces of truth in her oval face. Her life tells. She wasn't flat and lifeless. She was enjoying the cards, the food, the conversation. She always did. He never flattered himself that it was him, particularly, that she hurried to see each year, but she loved the single day of decadence that they always shared on December twentieth. Not the expenditure—she and Blake were both on healthy incomes and she could buy this sort of experience herself if she really wanted to—it was the low-key luxury of this restaurant, this day, that she really got off on.

She was the only woman he'd ever met who got more excited by *not* being flashy with his money. By being as tastefully understated as she always was. It suited her down to the ground. Elegant instead of glitzy, all that dark hair twisted in a lazy knot on top of her head with what looked like bamboo spears holding it all together. The way her hands occasionally ran across the fabric of her tailored skirt told him she enjoyed how the fabric felt against her skin. That was why she wore it; not for him, or any other man. Not because it hugged the intriguing curve of her thighs almost indecently. The money Audrey spent on fashion was about recognising her equal in a quality product.

Whether she knew that or not.

Which was why he struggled so badly with Blake's protestations that Audrey was cool with his marital... excursions. He got that they didn't have the most conventional of marriages—definitely a meeting of minds—but she just didn't strike him as someone who would tolerate the cheapening of her relationship through his playing around. Because, if nothing else, Blake's sleeping around reflected on her.

And Audrey Devaney was anything but cheap.

'Oliver?'

He refocused to find those sapphire eyes locked hard on his. 'Sorry. Raise.'

She smiled at his distraction and then flicked her focus back down to her cards, leaving him staring at those long, down-curved lashes.

*Did* she know that her husband hooked up with someone else the moment she left town? Did that bother her? Or did she fabricate trips specifically to give Blake the opportunity, to give herself necessary distance from his infidelity, and preserve the amazing dignity that she wore like one of her silk suits. He'd never got the slightest sense that she evened the score while she travelled. Not that he'd necessarily know if she did—she would be as discreet about that as she was about the other details of her life—but her work ethic was nearly as solid as her friendship. And, as the lucky beneficiary of her unwavering loyalty as a friend, he knew that if Audrey was in Asia working then that was exactly what she'd be doing.

Working her silk-covered butt off.

And, if she wasn't, he'd know it. When it came to her, his radar was fine-tuned for the slightest hint that she was operating on the same wavelength as her husband.

Because if Audrey Devaney was *on* the market, then he was *in* the market.

No matter the price. No matter the terms. No matter what he'd believed his whole life about fidelity. He'd had enough hot, restless nights after waking from one of his dreams—riddled with passion and guilt and Audrey up against the cold glass of the window facing out over Victoria Harbour—to know what his body wanted.

'Call.' She tossed a cluster of M&M's onto the pile, interrupting the dangerous direction of his thoughts.

But he also knew himself pretty well. He knew that sex was the great equaliser and that reducing a woman that he admired and liked so much to the subject of one of his cheap fantasies was just his subconscious' way of dealing with the unfamiliar territory.

Territory in which he found himself fixated on the only woman he knew who was *genuinely* too good for him.

'Your game.' Oliver tossed aces and jacks purely for the pleasure of seeing the flush Audrey couldn't contain. The pleasure that spilled out over the edges of her usual propriety. She loved to win. She loved to beat him, particularly.

And he loved to watch her enjoy it.

She flipped a trio of fours on top of the mound of M&M's triumphantly and her perfectly made-up skin practically glowed with pleasure. Instantly, he wondered if that was what she'd look like if he pushed this table aside and pressed her back into the sofa with his lips against that confident smile and his thigh between hers.

His body cheered the very thought.

'Rematch,' he demanded, forcing his brain clean of smut. Pretty sad when throwing a card game was about as erotic as any dream he could conjure up. 'Double or nothing.'

She tipped her head back to laugh and that knot piled on the top and decorated with a bit of stolen airport tinsel wobbled dangerously. If he kept the humour coming maybe the whole thing would come tumbling down and he'd have another keeper memory for his pathetic fantasy-stalker collection.

'Sure, while you're throwing your chocolates away...'

She slipped off her shoes and pulled slim legs up onto the sofa as Oliver dealt another hand and, again, he was struck by how down to earth she was. And how innocent. This was not the relaxed, easy expression of a woman who knew her husband was presently shacked up with someone that wasn't his wife.

No question.

Which meant his best friend was a liar as well as an adulterer. And a fool, too, for cheating on the most amazing woman either of them had ever known. Just *wasting* the beautiful soul he'd been gifted by whatever fate sent Audrey in Blake's direction instead of his own all those years ago.

But where fate was vague and indistinct, that out-of-place rock weighing down her left hand was very real, and though her husband was progressively sleeping his way through Sydney, Audrey wasn't following suit.

Because that ring meant something to her.

Just as fidelity meant something to him.

Perhaps that was the great attraction. Audrey was moral and compassionate, and her integrity was rooted as firmly as the mountains that surged up out of the ocean all around them to form the islands of Hong Kong where they both flew to meet each December twentieth. Splitting the difference between Sydney and Shanghai.

And he was enormously drawn to that integrity, even as he cursed it. Would he be as drawn to her if she was playing the field like her selfish husband? Or was he only obsessed with her because he knew he couldn't have her?

That was more his playbook.

Just because he didn't do unfaithful didn't mean he was pro-commitment. The whole Tiffany thing was really a kind of retirement. He'd given up on finding the woman he secretly dreamed was out there for him and settled for one that would let him do whatever he wanted, whenever he wanted and look good doing it.

And clearly even that wasn't meant to be.

'Come on, Harmer. Man up.'

His eyes shot up, fearing for one irrational moment that she'd read the direction of his inappropriate thoughts.

'It's just one game,' she teased. 'I'm sure you'll take me on the next one.'

She was probably right. He'd do what he did every Christmas: give enough to keep her engaged and entertained, and take enough to keep her colour high with indignation. To keep her coming back for more. Coming back to him. In the name of her cheating bastard of a husband who only ever visited him when he was travelling alone—though he'd be sure to put an end to that, now—and who took carnal advantage of every opportunity when Audrey was out of the country.

But, just as he suppressed his natural distaste for Blake's infidelity so that he could maintain the annual Christmas lunch with his best friend's wife, so he would keep Blake's secret.

Not only because he didn't want to hurt gentle Audrey.

And not because he condoned Blake's behaviour in the slightest—though he really, really didn't.

And not because he enjoyed being some kind of confessional for the man he'd stood beside at his wedding.

No, he'd keep Blake's secret because keeping it meant he got to have Audrey in his life. If he shared what he knew she'd leave Blake, and if she left Blake Oliver knew he'd never see her again. And it was only as he saw her friendship potentially slipping away like a landslide that he realised how very much he valued—and needed—it.

And her.

So he did what he did every year. He concentrated on Audrey and on enjoying what little time they had together this one day of the year. He feasted like the glutton he was on her conversation and her presence and he pushed everything else into the background where it belonged.

He had all year to deal with that. And with his conscience.

He stretched his open palm across the table, the shuffled cards upturned on it. As she took the pack, her soft fingers brushed against his palm, birthing a riot of sensation in his nerve endings. And he boxed those sensations up, too, for dealing with later, when he didn't have this amazing woman sitting opposite him with her all-seeing eyes focused squarely on him.

'Your deal.'

# CHAPTER TWO

*December 20th, three years ago*
*Qīngtíng Restaurant, Hong Kong*

BEHIND HER BACK, Audrey pressed the soft flesh of her wrists to the glassy chill of the elevator's mirrored wall, desperate to cool the blazing blood rushing through her arteries. To quell the excited flush she feared stained her cheeks from standing this close to Oliver Harmer in such a tight space.

You'd think twelve months would be enough time to steel her resolve and prepare herself.

Yet here she was, entirely rattled by the anticipation of a simple farewell kiss. It never was more than a socially appropriate graze. Barely more than an air-kiss. Yet she still felt the burn of his lips on her cheek as though last year's kiss were a moment—and not a full year—ago.

She was a teenager again, around Oliver. All breathless and hot and hormonal. Totally fixated on him for the short while she had his company. It would have been comic if it weren't also so terribly mortifying. And it was way too easy to indulge the feelings this one day of the year. It felt dangerous and illicit to let the emotions even slightly off the leash. Thank goodness she was old enough now to fake it like a seasoned professional.

In public, anyway.

Oliver glanced down and smiled at her in that strange, searching way he had, a half-unwrapped DVD boxed set in his hands. She gave him her most careful smile back, took a deep breath and then refocused on the light descending the crowded panel of elevator buttons.

*Fifty-nine, fifty-eight...*

She wasn't always so careful. She caught herself two weeks ago wondering what her best man would think of tonight's dress instead of her husband. But she'd rationalised it by saying that Oliver's taste in women—and, by implication, his taste in their wardrobes—was far superior to Blake's and so taking trouble to dress well was important for a man who hosted her in a swanky Hong Kong restaurant each year.

Blake, on the other hand, wouldn't notice if she came to the dinner table dressed in a potato sack.

He used to notice—back in the day, nine years ago—when she'd meet him and Oliver at a restaurant in something flattering. Or sheer-cut. Or reinforcing. Back then, appreciation would colour Blake's skin noticeably. Or maybe it just seemed more pronounced juxtaposed with the blank indifference on Oliver's face. Oliver, who barely even glanced at her until she was seated behind a table and modestly secured behind a menu.

Yet, paradoxically, she had him to thank for the evolution of her fashion sense because his disdain was a clear litmus test if something was *too* flattering, *too* sheer-cut. *Too* reinforcing.

It was all there in the careful nothing of his expression.

People paid top dollar for that kind of fashion advice. Oliver gifted her with it for free.

Yeah...his *gift*. That felt so much better on the soul than his *judgement*. And seasonally appropriate, too.

This year's outfit was a winner. And while she missed the disguised scrutiny of his greenish-brown gaze—the visual caress that usually sustained her all year—the warm wash of his approval was definitely worth it. She glanced at herself in the elevator's mirrored walls and tried to see herself as Oliver might. Slim, professional, well groomed.

Weak at the knees with utterly inappropriate anticipation.

*Forty-five, forty-four...*

'What time is your flight in the morning?' His deep voice honey-rumbled in the small space.

Her answer was more breath than speech. 'Eight.'

*Excellent. Resorting to small talk.* But this was always how it went at the end. As though they'd flat run out of other things to talk about. Entirely possible given the gamut of topics they covered during their long, long lunch-that-became-dinner, and because she was usually emotionally and intellectually drained from so many hours sitting across from a man she longed to see but really struggled to be around.

It was only one day.

Twelve hours, really. That was all she had to get through each year and wasn't a big ask of her body. The rest of the year she had no trouble suppressing the emotions. She used the long flight home to marshal all the sensations back into that tightly lidded place she kept them so that she disembarked the plane in Sydney as strong as when she'd left Australia.

She'd invited Blake along this year—pure survival, hoping her husband's presence would force her wayward thoughts back into safer territory—but not only had he declined, he'd looked horrified at the suggestion. Which made no sense because he liked to catch up with Oliver whenever he was travelling in Asia, himself. Least he used to.

In fact, it made about as little sense as the not-so-subtle way Oliver changed the subject every time she mentioned

Blake. As if he was trying to distance himself from the only person they had in common.

And without Blake in common, really what did they have?

*Twenty-seven, twenty-six, twenty-five...*

Breath hissed out of her in a long, controlled yoga sigh and she willed her fluttering pulse to follow its lead. But that persistent flutter was still entirely fixated on the gorgeous, expensive aftershave Oliver wore and the heat coming off his big body and it seemed to fibrillate faster the closer to the ground floor they got.

And they were so close, now.

Ultimately, it didn't matter what her body did when in Oliver's immediate proximity—how her breath tightened, or her mouth dried or her heart squeezed—that was like Icarus hoping his wings wouldn't melt as he flew towards the sun.

There was nothing she could do about the fundamental rules of biology. All that mattered was that it didn't show on the outside.

On pain of death.

Tonight she'd been the master of her anatomy. Giving nothing away. So she only had to last these final few moments and she'd be away, speeding through the streets of Hong Kong en route to her own hotel room. Her cool, safe, empty bed. The sleepless night that was bound to follow. And the airport bright and early in the morning.

She should really get the red-eye next year.

It was impossible to know whether the lurch in her stomach was due to the arrest of the elevator's rapid descent or because she knew what was coming next. The elegant doors seemed to gather their wits a moment before opening.

Audrey did the same.

They whooshed open and she matched Oliver's footfalls out through the building's plush foyer onto the street, then turned on a smile and extended a hand as a taxi pulled up from the nearby rank to attend them.

'Any message for Blake?'

She always kept something aside for this exact moment. Something strong and obstructive in case her body decided to hurl itself at him and embarrass them all. Invariably Blake-related because that was about the safest territory the two of them had. Blake or work. Not to mention the fact that reference to her husband was usually one of the only things that made a dent in the hormonal surge that swilled around them when they stood this close.

The swampy depths of his eyes darkened for the briefest of moments as he took her hand in his large one. 'No. Thank you.'

*Odd.* Blake hadn't had one, either. Which was a first…

But her curiosity about that half-hidden flash of anger lasted a mere nanosecond in the face of the heat soaking from his hand into the one he hadn't released anywhere nearly as swiftly as she'd offered it. He held it—no caresses, nothing that would raise an eyebrow for anyone watching—and used it to pull her towards him for their annual Christmas air-kiss.

Her blood surged against its own current; the red cells rushing downstream to pool in fingers that tingled at Oliver's touch stampeding against the foolish ones that surged, upstream, to fill the lips that she knew full well weren't going to get to touch his.

She thrilled for this moment and hated it at the same time because it was never enough. Yet of course it had to be. The sharp, expensive tang of his cologne washed over her catgut-tight senses as he leaned down and brushed his lips against her cheek. A little further back from last year. A little lower, too. Close enough to her pulse to feel it pounding under her skin.

Barely enough to even qualify as a kiss. But ten times as swoon-worthy as any real kiss she'd ever had.

Hormones.

Talk about mind-altering chemicals…

'Until next year,' he breathed against her ear as he withdrew.

'I will.'

*Give my regards to Blake.* That was what usually came after 'the kiss' and she'd uttered her response before her foggy brain caught up to the fact that he hadn't actually asked it of her this year. Again, odd. So her next words were stammered and awkward. Definitely not the cool, calm and composed Audrey she usually liked to finish her visit on.

'Well, goodbye, then. Thank you for lunch.'

Ugh. Lame.

Calling their annual culinary marathon 'lunch' was like suggesting that the way Oliver made her feel was 'warm'. Right now her body blazed with all the unspent chemistry from twelve hours in his company and her head spun courtesy of the shallow breathing of the past few minutes. Embarrassed heat blazed up the back of her neck and she slipped quickly into the waiting taxi before it bloomed fully in her face.

Oliver stood on the footpath, his hand raised in farewell as she pressed back against the headrest and the cab moved away.

'Wait!'

She lurched against her seat belt and suddenly Oliver was hauling the door open again. For one totally crazy, breathless heartbeat she thought he might have pulled her into his arms. And she would have gone into them. Unflinchingly.

But he didn't.

*Of course he didn't.*

'Audrey—'

She shoved her ritualistic in-taxi decompression routine down into the gap between the seat back and cushion and presented him with her most neutral, questioning expression.

'I just… I wanted to say…'

A dozen indecipherable expressions flitted across his expression but finally resolved into something that looked like pain. Grief.

'Merry Christmas, Audrey. I'll see you next year.'

The anticlimax was breath-stealing in its severity and so her words were little more than a disenchanted whisper.

'Merry Christmas, Oliver.'

'If you ever need me…need anything. Call me.' His hazel eyes implored. 'Any time, day or night. Don't hesitate.'

'Okay,' she pledged, though had no intention of taking him up on it. Oliver Harmer and The Real World did not mix. They existed comfortably in alternate realities and her flight to and from Hong Kong was the inter-dimensional transport. In this reality he was the first man—the only man—she'd ever call if she were in trouble. But back home…

Back home she knew her life was too beige to need his help and even if she did, she wouldn't let herself call him.

The taxi pulled away again and Audrey resumed decompression. Her breath eased out in increments until her heart settled down to a heavy, regular beat and her skin warmed back up to room temperature.

*Done.*

Another year survived. Another meeting endured in her husband's name and hopefully with her dignity fully intact.

And only three hundred and sixty-five days until she saw Oliver Harmer again.

Long, confusing days.

# CHAPTER THREE

*December 20th, two years ago*
*Qīngtíng Restaurant, Hong Kong*

OLIVER STARED OUT at the midnight sky, high enough above the flooding lights of Hong Kong to actually see a few stars, and did his best to ignore the screaming lack of attention being paid to him by Qīngtíng's staff as they closed up the restaurant for the night.

The arms crossed firmly across his chest were the only thing keeping his savaged heart in his chest cavity, and the beautifully wrapped gift crushed in his clenched fist was the only thing stopping him from slamming it into the wall.

*She hadn't come.*

For the first time in years, Audrey hadn't come.

# CHAPTER FOUR

*December 20th, last year*
*Obsiblue prawn and caviar with Royale Cabanon Oyster*
*and Yuzu*

'YOU'RE LUCKY I'M even here.'

The rumbled accusation filtered through the murmur of low conversation and the chink of expensive silverware on Qīngtíng's equally expensive porcelain. Audrey turned towards Oliver's neutral displeasure, squared the shoulders of her cream linen jacket and smoothed her hands down her skirt.

'Yet here you are.'

A grunt lurched in Oliver's tanned throat where a business tie should have been holding his navy silk shirt appropriately together. Or at the very least some buttons. Benefit of being such a regular patron—or maybe so rich—niceties like dress code didn't seem to apply to him.

'Guess I'm slow to learn,' he said, still dangerously calm. 'Or just naively optimistic.'

'Not so naive. I'm here, aren't I?'

'You don't look too pleased about it.'

'Your email left me little choice. I didn't realise how proficient you'd become in emotional blackmail.'

'It wasn't blackmail, Audrey. I just wanted to know if

you were coming. To save me wasting another day and the flight from Shanghai.'

Shame battled annoyance. Yes, she'd stood him up last year, but she found it hard to imagine a man like Oliver left alone and dateless in a flash restaurant for very long. Especially at Christmas. Especially in a city full of home-sick expats. She was sure he wouldn't have withered away from lack of company.

'And playing the dead best friend card seemed equal to your curiosity, did it?'

Because that was the only reason she was here at all. The relationship he'd had with her recently passed husband. And she'd struggled to shake the feeling that she needed to provide some closure for Oliver on that friendship.

His hazel eyes narrowed just a hint in that infuriating, corporate, too-cool-for-facial-expression way he had. But he didn't bite. Instead he just stared at her, almost daring her to go on. Daring her, just as much, to hold his glower.

'They got new carpet,' she announced pointlessly, thrilled for an excuse not to let him enslave her gaze. Styl-ised and vibrant dragonflies decorated the floor where once obscure oriental patterns had previously lain. She sank the pointed tip of her cream shoe into the plush opulence and watched it disappear into Weihei Province's best hand-tufted weave. 'Nice.'

'Gerard got another Michelin.' He shrugged. 'New car-pet seemed a reasonable celebration.'

Somehow, Oliver managed to make her failure to know that one of Hong Kong's most elite restaurants had re-carpeted sound like a personal failure on her part.

'Mrs Audrey...'

Audrey suppressed the urge to correct that title as she turned and took the extended hand of the maître d' between her own. 'Ming-húa, lovely to see you again.'

'You look beautiful,' Ming-húa said, raising her hand to his lips. 'We missed you last Christmas.'

Oliver shot her a sideways look as they were shepherded towards their customary part of the restaurant. The end where the Chinese version of Christmas decorations were noticeably denser. They racked up a bill this one day of the year large enough to warrant the laying on of extra festive bling and the discreet removal of several other tables, yet, this year, more tables than ever seemed to have been sacrificed. It left them with complete privacy, ensconced in the western end of the restaurant between the enormous indoor terrarium filled with verdant water-soaked plants and fluorescent dragonflies, and the carpet-to-ceiling reinforced window that served as the restaurant's outer wall.

Beyond the glass, Victoria Harbour and the high-tech sparkle and glint of hundreds more towering giants just like this side of the shore. Behind the glass, the little haven that Audrey had missed so badly last Christmas. Tranquil, private and filled with the kind of gratuitous luxury a girl really should indulge in only once a year.

Emotional sanctuary.

The sanctuary she'd enjoyed for the past five years.

Minus the last one.

And Oliver Harmer was a central part of all that gratuitous luxury. Especially looking like he did today. She didn't like to notice his appearance—he had enough ego all by himself without her appreciation adding to it—but, here, it was hard to escape; wherever she looked, a polished glass surface of one kind or another offered her a convenient reflection of some part of him. Parts that were infinitely safer facing away from her.

Chilled Cristal sat—as it always did—at the centre of the small table between two large, curved sofas. The first and only furniture she'd ever enjoyed that was actually worthy of the name *lounge*. Certainly, by the end of the day they'd both be sprawled across their respective sides, bodies sated with the best food and drink, minds saturated with good conversation, a year's worth of catching up all done and dusted.

At least that was how it normally went.

But things weren't normal any more.

Suddenly the little space she'd craved so much felt claustrophobic and the chilled Cristal looked like something from a cheesy seduction scene. And the very idea that she could do anything other than perch nervously on the edge of her sofa for the next ten or twelve hours...?

Ludicrous.

'So what are you hunting this trip?' Oliver asked, no qualms whatsoever about flopping down into his lounge, snagging up a quarter-filled flute on the way down. So intently casual she wondered if he'd practised the manoeuvre. As he settled back his white shirt stretched tight across his torso and his dark trousers hiked up to reveal ankles the same tanbark colour as his throat. 'Stradivarius? Guarneri?'

'A 1714 Testore cello,' she murmured. 'Believed to now be in South East Asia.'

'Now?'

'It moves around a lot.'

'Do they know you're looking for it?'

'I have to assume so. Hence its air miles.'

'More fool them trying to outrun you. Don't they know you always get your man...or instrument?'

'I doubt they know me at all. You forget, I do all the legwork but someone else busts up the syndicates. My job relies on my contribution being anonymous.'

'Anonymous,' he snorted as he cut the tip off one of the forty-dollar cigars lying on a tray beside the champagne. 'I'd be willing to wager that a specialist with an MA in identification of antique stringed instruments is going to be of much more interest to the bad guys than a bunch of

Interpol thugs with a photograph and a GPS location in their clammy palms.'

'The day my visa gets inexplicably denied then I'll start believing you. Until then…' She helped herself to the Cristal. 'Enough about my work. How is yours going? Still rich?'

'Stinking.'

'Still getting up the noses of your competitors?'

'Right up in their sinuses, in fact.'

Despite everything, it was hard not to respond to the genuine glee Oliver got from irritating his corporate rivals. He wasted a fair bit of money on moves designed to exasperate. Though, not a waste at all if it kept their focus conveniently on what he *wasn't* doing. A reluctant smile broke free.

'I was wondering if I'd be seeing that today.' His eyes flicked to her mouth for the barest of moments. 'I've missed it.'

That was enough to wipe the smile clean from her face. 'Yeah, well, there's been a bit of an amusement drought since Blake's funeral.'

Oliver flinched but buried it behind a healthy draw from his champagne. 'No doubt.'

Well… *Awkward*…

'So how are you doing?' He tried again.

She shrugged. 'Fine.'

'And how are you really doing?'

Seriously? He wanted to do this? Then again, they talked about Blake every year. He was their connection, after all. Their *only* true connection. Which made being here now that Blake was gone even weirder. She should have just stayed home. Maybe they could have just done this by phone.

'The tax stuff was a bit of a nightmare and the house was secured against the business so that wasn't fun to disentangle, but I got there.'

He blinked at her. 'And personally?'

'Personally my husband's dead. What do you want me to say?'

All the champagne chugging in the world wasn't going to disguise the three concerned lines that appeared between his brows. 'Are you…coping?'

'Are you asking me about my finances?'

'Actually no. I'm asking you how you're doing. You, Audrey.'

'And I said *fine*.'

Both hands went up, one half filled with champagne flute. 'Okay. Next subject.'

And what would that be? Their one reason for continuing to see each other had gone trundling down a conveyor belt at the crematorium. Not that he'd remember that.

*Why weren't you at your best friend's funeral?* How was that for another subject? But she wouldn't give him the satisfaction.

Unfortunately, for them both, Oliver looked as uninspired as she did on the conversation front.

She pushed to her feet. 'Maybe this wasn't such a—'

'Here we go!' Ming-húa appeared flanked by two serving staff carrying the first amuse-bouche of their marine-themed Christmas degustation. 'Obsiblue prawn and caviar with Royale Cabanon Oyster and Yuzu.'

Audrey got 'prawn', 'caviar' and 'oyster' and not much else. But wasn't that kind of the point with degustation—to over-stimulate your senses and not be overly bothered by what things were or used to be?

Culinary adventure.

Pretty much the only place in her life she risked adventure.

She sank politely back onto her sofa. It took the highly trained staff just moments to place their first course *just so* and then they were alone again.

Oliver ignored the food and slid a small gift-wrapped parcel across the table.

Audrey stared at the patched-up wrapping. Best he was prepared to do after she'd stood him up? 'Um…'

'I don't expect anything in return, Audrey.'

Did he read everyone this well? 'I didn't imagine we'd be doing gifts this year.'

'This was from last year.'

She paused a moment longer, then pulled the small parcel towards her. But she didn't open it because opening it meant something. She set it aside, instead, smiling tightly.

Oliver pinned her with his intense gaze. 'We've been friends for years, Audrey. We've done this for years, every Christmas. Are you telling me you were only here for Blake?'

The slightest hint of hurt diluted the hazel of his eyes. One of the vibrant dragonflies flitting around the enormous terrarium matched the colour exactly.

She gifted him with the truth. 'It feels odd to be doing this with him gone.'

She didn't want to say *wrong*. But it had always felt vaguely wrong. Or her own reaction to Oliver certainly had. Wrong and dishonest because she'd kept it so secret and close to her heart.

'Everything is different now. But our friendship doesn't have to change. Spending time with you was never just about courtesy to a mate's wife. As far as I'm concerned we're friends, too.'

*Pfff.* Meaningless words. 'I missed you at *your mate's* funeral.'

A deep flush filled the hollow where his tie should have been. 'I was sorry not to be there.'

Uh-huh.

'Economic downturn made the flight unaffordable, I guess.' They would spend four times that cost on today's meals. But one of Oliver's strengths had always been courage under fire. He pressed his lips together and remained silent. 'Or was it just a really busy week at the office?'

She'd called. She knew exactly where he was while they'd buried her husband. 'Or did you not get my messages in time?'

All eight of them.

'Audrey...' The word practically hissed out of him.

'Oliver?'

'You know I would have been there if I could. Did you get the flowers I arranged?'

'The half-a-boutique of flowers? Yes. They were crammed in every corner of the chapel. And they were lovely,' honesty compelled her to admit. And also her favourites. 'But they were just flowers.'

'Look, Audrey, I can see you're upset. Can I please just ask you to trust that I had my reasons, good reasons, not to fly back to Sydney and that I had my own private memorial for my old friend back home in Shanghai—' Audrey didn't miss the emphasis on *'old'* friend '—complete with a half-bottle of Chivas. So Blake had two funerals that day.'

Why was this so hard? She shouldn't still care.

She shouldn't still remember so vividly the way she'd craned her neck from inside the funeral car to see if Oliver was walking in the procession of mourners. Or the way she'd only half attended to the raft of well-wishers squeezing her hand after the service because she was too busy wondering how she'd missed him. It was only later as she wrote thank-you cards to the names collected by the funeral attendants that she'd finally accepted the truth.

Oliver hadn't come.

Blake's best friend—their best man—hadn't come to his funeral.

That particular truth had been bitter, but she'd been too swamped in the chaos of new widowhood to be curious as to why it hurt so much. Or to imagine Oliver finding a private way of farewelling his old mate. Like downing a half-bottle of whisky.

'He always did love a good label,' she acknowledged.

A little too fondly as it turned out since Blake's thirst for good liquor was deemed a key contributor to the motor vehicle accident that took his life. But since her husband sitting in his den enjoying a sizeable glass or three with the evening newspaper had given Audrey the space and freedom to pursue things she enjoyed, she really couldn't complain.

The natural pause in the uncomfortable conversation was a cue to both of them to eat, and the tart seafood amuse-bouche was small enough that it was over in just mouthfuls.

Behind her, the gentle buzz of dragonfly wings close to glass drew her focus. She turned to study the collection that gave the restaurant its name. There were over one hundred species in Hong Kong—vibrant and fluorescent, large and small—and Qīngtíng kept an immaculate and stunning community of them in the specially constructed habitat.

She discreetly took several deep breaths to get her wayward feelings under control. 'Every year, I forget how amazing this is.'

And, every year, she envied the insects and pitied them, equally. Their captive life was one of luxury, with every conceivable need met. Their lives were longer and easier than their wild counterparts and neither their wetland nor food source ever dried up. Yet the glass boundaries of their existence was immutable. New arrivals battered softly against it until they eventually stopped trying and they accepted their luxurious fate.

Ultimately, didn't everyone?

'Give him a chance and the dragonfly curator will talk your ear off with the latest developments in invertebrate husbandry.'

His tone drew her eyes back. 'I thought you only flew down for the day? When did you have a chance to meet Qīngtíng's dragonfly guy?'

'Last Christmas. I unexpectedly found myself with time on my hands.'

Because she hadn't come.

The shame washed in again. 'It was…too soon. I couldn't leave Australia. And Blake was gone.'

He stared at her. Contemplating. 'Which one of those do you want to go with?'

Heat rushed up her neck.

'They're all valid.' His silence only underscored her lies. She took a deep breath. 'I'm sorry I didn't come last year, Oliver. I should have had more courage.'

'Courage?'

'To tell you that it was the last time I'd be coming.'

He flopped back in his chair. 'Is that what you've come to say now?'

It was. Although, saying it aloud seemed to be suddenly impossible. She nodded instead.

'We could have done that by phone. It would have been cheaper for you.'

'I had the Testore—'

'You could have come and not told me you were here. Like you did in Shanghai.'

Every muscle tightened up.

*Busted.*

She generally did her best to deal with Shanghai contacts outside Shanghai for a very specific reason—it was Harmer-country, and going deep into Oliver's own turf wasn't something she'd been willing to risk let alone tell him about. But how could he possibly know the population had swelled to twenty-five-million-and-one just that once? She asked him exactly that.

His eyes held hers. 'I have my sources.'

And why exactly were his sources pointing in her direction?

'Before you get too creeped out,' he went on, 'it was social media. Your status listed your location as the People's Square, so I knew you were in town.'

Ugh. Stupid too-smart phones. 'You didn't message me.'

'I figured if you wanted to see me you would have let me know.'

*Oh.* Sneaking in and out of China's biggest city like a thief was pathetic enough, but being so stupidly caught out just made her look—and feel—like a child. 'It was a flying visit,' she croaked. 'I was hunting a Paraguayan harp.'

Lord. *Not making it better.*

'It doesn't matter, that's in the past. I want to know why you won't be returning in the future.'

Discomfort gnawed at her intestines. 'I can't keep flying here indefinitely, Oliver. Can't we just say it's been great and let it go?'

He processed that for a moment. 'Do all your friends have best-by dates?'

His perception had her buzzing as furiously as the dragonflies. 'Is that what we are? Friends?'

'I thought so.' His eyes narrowed. 'I never got the sense that you were here under sufferance. You certainly seemed very comfortable helping me spend my money.'

'Oliver—'

'What's really going on, Audrey? What's the problem?'

'Blake's gone,' she pointed out needlessly on a great expulsion of breath. 'Me continuing to come and see you… What would be the point?'

'To catch up. To see each other.'

'Why would we do that?'

'Because friends nurture their relationships.'

'Our relationship was built on someone who's not here any more.'

He blinked at her—twice—and his perfect lips gaped. 'That might be how it started but it's not like that any longer.' An ocean of doubt swilled across the back of his gaze, though. 'I met you about six minutes before Blake did, if you recall. Technically, I think that means our friendship pre-dates Blake.'

That had been an excruciating six minutes, writhing under the intensity of the sexiest man she'd ever met, until his infinitely more ordinary friend had wandered into the Sydney bar. Blake with his narrower shoulders, his harmless smile and his non-challenging conversation. She'd practically swamped the man with her attention purely on reactive grounds, to crawl out from under Oliver's blistering microscope.

She knew when she was batting above her average and thirty seconds in his exclusive company told her Oliver Harmer was major league. Majorly gorgeous, majorly bright and majorly bored if he was entertaining himself by flirting with her.

'That doesn't count. You only spoke to me to pass the time until Blake turned up.'

He weighed something up. 'What makes you think I wasn't laying groundwork?'

'For Blake?'

His snort drew a pair of glances from across the room. 'For me. Blake's always been quite capable of doing his own dirty work...' As if it suddenly occurred to him that they were speaking of the dead, his words petered off. 'Anyway, as soon as he walked in the room you were captivated. I knew when I'd been bested.'

What would Oliver say if he knew she'd clung to Blake's conversation specifically to avoid having to engage with his more handsome friend again? Or if she confessed that she'd been aware of every single move Oliver made until the moment she left her phone number with Blake and fled out into the Australian night.

He'd probably laugh.

'I'm sure it did no permanent damage to your self-esteem,' she gritted.

'I had to endure his gloating for a week. It wasn't every day that he managed to steal out from under me a woman that I—' His teeth snapped shut.

'A woman that what?'

'Any woman at all, really. You were a first.'

She shook her head. 'Always so insufferable. *That's* why I gave my phone number to him and not you.'

That and the fact she always had been a coward.

He settled back into his sofa. 'Imagine how different things would be if you'd given it to me that day.'

'Oh, please. You would have bored of me within hours.'

'Who says?'

'It's just sport for you, Oliver.'

'Again. Who says?'

'Your track record says. And Blake says.'

*Said.*

He sat forward. 'What did he say?'

Enough to make her wonder if something had gone down between the two friends. She hedged by shrugging. 'He cared about you. He wanted you to have what he had.'

The brown flecks amid the green of his iris seemed to shift amongst themselves. 'What did he have?'

'A stable relationship. Permanency. A life partner.'

Would he notice she didn't say 'love'?

'That's rich, coming from him.'

'What do you mean?'

He glanced around the room and shifted uncomfortably in his seat before bringing his sharp, intent gaze back to her. Colour stained the very edge of his defined jaw. Audrey reached up to press her hand to her topknot to stop the lot falling down with the angle of her head. The pins really weren't doing their job so she pulled them out and the entire arrangement slid free and down to her shoulders.

His expression changed, morphed, as she watched, from something pointed to something intentionally dull. 'Doesn't matter what I mean. Ancient history. I didn't realise old Blake had such passion in him.'

'Excuse me?'

'Such possession. I always got the impression that your marriage was as much a meeting of minds as anything else.'

Heat raced up from under her linen collar. *What's wrong, Oliver, can't imagine me inspiring passion in a man?* 'You hadn't seen us together for years,' she said, tightly.

Why was that?

'My business relies on my ability to read people, Audrey. I hung out with you guys a lot those few years before your wedding. Before I moved to Shanghai. The three amigos, remember? Plenty of opportunity to form an opinion.'

Did she remember…?

She remembered the long dinners, the brilliant, three-way conversations. She remembered Oliver stepping between her and some drunk morons in the street, once, while Blake flanked her on the *protected* side. She remembered how breathless she felt when Oliver would walk towards them out of the twilight shadows and how flat she felt when he walked away.

Yeah. She remembered.

'Then you must recall how partial Blake was to public displays of affection.' Oliver used to get so embarrassed by them, looking away like the fifth wheel that he was. Hard to imagine the confident man that he now was being discomposed by anything. 'Wasn't that sufficient demonstration of his feelings?'

'It was a demonstration all right. I always got the feeling that Blake specially reserved the displays of affection for when you were *in* public.'

Mortification added a few more degrees to the heat that was only just settling back under her jacket. Because that was essentially true. Behind closed doors they lived more like siblings. But what he probably didn't know was that Blake saved the PDAs up most particularly for when Oliver was there. Scent marking like crazy. As though he was subliminally picking up on the interest she was trying so very hard to disguise.

She breathed in past the tightness of her chest. 'Really, Oliver? That's what you want to do today? Take shots at a dead man?'

Anger settled between his brows. 'I want to just enjoy today. Enjoy your company. Like we used to.'

He slid the gift back across in front of her. 'And on that note, open it.'

She sat unmoved for a moment but the steely determination in his gaze told her that was probably entirely pointless. He was just as likely to open it for her.

She tore the wrapping off with more an annoyance she hoped he'd misread as impatience.

'It's a cigar.' And a pack of cards and M&M's. Just like three years ago. Her eyes lifted back to his. Resisted their pull. 'I don't smoke.'

'That's never stopped me.'

She struggled against the warm memory of Oliver letting her beat him at cards and believing she hadn't noticed. 'That was a great day.'

'My favourite Christmas.'

'Nearly Christmas.'

His dark head shook. 'December twenty-fifth has never compared to the twentieth.'

She sat back. 'What do you do on Christmas Day?'

'Work, usually.'

'You don't go home?'

'Do I go to my father's home? No.'

'What about your mum?'

'I fly her to me for Chinese New Year. A less loaded holiday.'

Audrey just stared.

'You're judging me,' he murmured.

'No. I'm trying to picture it.'

'Think about it. I can't go back to Sydney, I can't go to a girlfriend's place on Christmas without setting up the expectations of rings and announcements, and the office is nice and quiet.'

'So you work.'

'It's just another day. What do you do?'

'I do Christmas.' She shrugged.

But it wasn't anywhere near as exciting as flying to see Oliver. Or as tasty as whatever festive treat Qīngtíng had in store for her. And it didn't warm her for the rest of the year. It was roast dinners and eggnog and family and gifts that none of them needed and explaining ad nauseam every year why Blake wasn't there.

Here she'd got to split her focus between the beautiful skyline that was Hong Kong and Oliver. Depending on her mood.

Her eyes fell back on his gift. She picked up the cigar and clamped it between her teeth in a parody of him. Two seconds later she let it fall out again.

'Ugh. That's horrible.'

His laugh could have lit the other end with its warmth. 'You get used to it.'

'I can't imagine how.'

Yet somehow, while it tasted awful on her own lips, she caught herself deciding it might taste better on his. And then she had to fight not to stare there. Oliver made that a whole lot harder by leaning forward, picking up the cigar where she'd dropped it, rolling it under his nose and then sliding the sealed end between his teeth. Pre-loved end first.

Something about the casual intimacy of that act, of him putting her saliva into his mouth so effortlessly—as if they were a long-term couple perfectly used to sharing bodily fluids—sent her heart racing, but she used every ounce of self-control she had to keep it from showing as he mouthed it from the right to the left.

Not the worst way to end your days if you were a cigar—
*Stop!*

Behind his easy smile his gaze grew unnaturally intent. And she grew inexplicably nervous.

'So,' he started, very much like one of his poker-plays, 'if we're not friends what are we?'

She choked slightly on her Cristal. 'Sorry?'

'I accept your assertion that we're not friends. But I wonder, then, what that means we are.'

Rabbit. Headlights. She knew it wasn't dignified and she knew exactly how that bunny felt, watching its fate career inevitably closer.

'Because there were two things that defined our relationship for me...' He used the word 'defined' as though it meant 'constrained'. 'One was that you were the wife of a friend. Now—tragically—no longer the case. And the other was that we were friends. Apparently also now no longer the case. So, tell me, Audrey—'

He leaned forward and swilled the liquid in his glass and his eyes locked on hard to hers.

'—where exactly does that leave us?'

# CHAPTER FIVE

*Lobster calamari tangle in braised southern ocean miniatures*

TENSION BALLED IN amongst the food in Audrey's stomach. She should have seen this coming. He wasn't a gazillionaire for nothing; the acute sharpness of his mind was one of the things that she…appreciated most about Oliver.

She flattened her skirt carefully. 'We're…acquaintances.'

Excellent. Yes. A nice neutral word.

He considered, nodded, and she thought she was safe. But then his head changed—mid-nod—into more of a shake. 'No, see that doesn't work for me. I wouldn't normally spend this much time—' or this much money, presumably '—on a mere acquaintance.'

'Associates?' She hid the croak in a swallow of champagne.

'Definitely not. That suggests we do business. And that's the last thing on my mind when we're together. It's why I enjoy our Christmases so much.'

'Then what do you suggest we are?'

He thought about that. 'Confidantes.'

He'd certainly shared a lot of himself with her, but they both knew it didn't go both ways.

'How about cohorts?' she parried.

He scrunched his nose. 'More consorts. In the literal sense.'

*No.* That just put way too vital an image in her head. 'Sidekicks?'

He laughed, but his eyes didn't. 'What about soulmates?'

The words. The implication. It was too much.

'Why are you doing this?' Audrey whispered, tight and tense.

'Doing what?'

What was it exactly? Flirting? Pressing? She stared at him and hoped her face wasn't as bleak as her voice. 'Stirring.'

He drained the last of the Cristal from his glass. 'I'm just trying to shake you free of the cold, impersonal place you put yourself in order to have this conversation.'

'I don't mean to be impersonal.' Or cold. Though that was a term she'd heard before courtesy of Blake. In his meaner moments.

'I know you don't, Audrey. That's the only reason I'm not mad at you. It's a survival technique.'

'Uh-huh...' She frowned in a way she hoped would cover the fact he was one hundred per cent right. 'And what am I surviving?'

'This day?' He stared, long and hard. 'Maybe me?'

'Don't flatter yourself.'

Four staff with exquisite timing arrived with the second seafood plate of the degustation experiences ahead of them. Two cleared the table and two more lay down matching shards of driftwood, decorated with glistening seaweed, and nested in it were a selection of oceanic morsels. A solitary lobster claw, calamari in a bed of roe, a fan of some kind of braised whitebait and—

Audrey leaned in for a good look. 'Is that krill?'

Oliver chuckled and it eased some of the tension that

hung as thick as the krill between them. 'Don't ask. Just taste.'

Whatever it was, it was magnificent. Weird texture on the tongue but one of the tastiest mouthfuls she'd ever had. Until she got to the lobster claw.

'Oh, my…'

'They've really outdone themselves with this one.'

The whole selection slid down way too easily with the frosty glass of Spanish Verdelho that had appeared in front of each of their dishes. But once there was nothing left on their driftwood but claw-husk and seaweed, conversation had no choice but to resume.

'Ask me how I know,' Oliver urged and then at her carefully blank stare he clarified. 'Ask me how I know what it is that you're doing.'

She took a deep slow breath. 'How do you know what I'm supposedly doing, Oliver?'

'I recognise it. From dealing with you the past five years. Eight if you want to go right back to the beginning.'

Oh, would that she could. The things she would do differently…

'I recognise it from keeping everything so carefully appropriate with you. From knowing exactly where the boundaries are and stopping with the tips of my shoes right on the line. From talking myself repeatedly into the fact that we're only friends.'

Audrey's heart hammered wildly. 'We are.'

He leapt on that. 'So now we *are* friends? Make up your mind.'

She couldn't help responding to the frustration leaching through between his words. 'I don't know what you want from me, Oliver.'

'Yes, you do.' He shifted forward again, every inch the predator. 'But you're in denial.'

'About what?'

'About what we really are.'

They couldn't be anything else. They just couldn't. 'There's no great mystery. You were my best man. You were my husband's closest friend.'

'I stopped being Blake's friend three years ago, Audrey.'

The pronouncement literally stunned her into silence. Her mouth opened and closed silently in protest. She knew something had gone down between them but…that long ago?

She picked up the M&M's. 'This long?'

'Just after that.' He guessed her next question. 'Friendships change. People change.'

'Why didn't you tell me?' she whispered. *And why hadn't Blake?* He knew that she saw Oliver whenever she went to Hong Kong. Why the hell wouldn't her husband tell her not to come?

He took a long breath. 'I didn't tell you because you would have stopped coming.'

Only the gentle murmur of conversation, the clink of silverware on plates and the hum of dragonfly wings interrupted the long, shocking silence. There was so much more in that sentence than the sum of the words. Two staff materialised behind them, unobtrusively cleared away the driftwood and shell remnants and left a small palate cleanser in their place. Then they were alone again.

'So, my comments today can't have been a surprise, then.' She braved her way carefully through the next moments. 'You knew I was going to end it.'

'Doesn't mean I'm going to acquiesce politely and let you walk off into the sunset.'

Frustration strung tight and painful across her sternum. 'Why, Oliver?'

He swapped the cigar from the left side of his mouth to the right. 'Because I don't want to. Because I like what we do and I like how I feel when we do it. And because I think you're kidding yourself if you don't admit you feel the same.'

The challenge—and the truth—hung out there, heavy and unignorable.

A nervous habit from her childhood came screaming back and, even though she knew she was doing it, she was helpless to stop her palms from rubbing back and forth along her thighs.

In desperation, she spooned up the half-melted sorbet and its icy bite shocked the breath right back into her. Oliver waited out her obvious ploy.

'I—'

Lord, was this wise? Couldn't she just lie and be done with it? But this was Oliver staring at her with such intensity and it didn't matter that he only saw her for ten hours a year, he could read her better than she could read herself.

'I enjoy seeing you, too,' she sighed. 'You know I do.'

'So why end it?'

'What will people say?'

Was that the first time she'd ever surprised him? Maybe so, given how unfamiliar that expression seemed on his face. 'What people?'

'Any people.'

'They'll say we're two friends having lunch.'

And dinner and sometimes a late supper to finish up with, but that was besides the point. 'They'll say I'm a widow moving on before her husband's scent has even left the house.'

'It's just lunch, Audrey. Once a year. At *Christmas*.'

'As if the people I'm worried about would give a rat's what season it is.'

'What do you care what they say? You and I will both know the truth.'

She shot a puff of air between her lips. 'Spoken just like

a man with more money than a small nation. You might not care about yours but reputations *mean* something to me.'

He shook his head. 'How is it any different than what we've been doing the past five years? Meeting, spending the day together.'

'The difference is Blake isn't here any more. He was the reason I came.'

He made it legitimate.

Now it was just…dangerous.

'Most women would be worried about *that* getting to the gossips. A married woman flying around the world to see a man that's not her husband. But you didn't care about it before you lost Blake—why do you care now?'

'Because now I'm—'

She floundered and he bent in closer to study her. 'You're what? The only thing that's changed in our relationship is your marital status.'

Her body locked up hard as awareness flooded his eyes.

'Is that it, Audrey? You're worried now because you're single?'

'How will it look?'

'You're a widow. No one will give a toss what you do or who you see. There's no hint of scandal for them to inhale.' But as she stared at him in desperate silence the awareness consolidated down into acute realisation. 'Or are you more concerned about how it will look, *to me*?'

Her pulse pounded against her throat. 'I don't want to give the wrong impression.'

'What impression is that?' Cool and oh, so careful.

'That I'm here because… That we're…'

He flopped back against the plush sofa, the cigar hanging limply from his mouth. 'That you're interested?'

'That I'm offering.'

Expressions chased across his face then like a classic

flicker-show and finally settled on heated disbelief. 'It's lunch, Audrey. Not foreplay.'

*That* word on *those* lips was all it took; her mind filled then with every carnal thought about him she'd ever suppressed. They burst out just as surely as if someone took the lid off the tank holding all those dragonflies captive, releasing them to fill the room and ricochet off the walls. It took all her concentration to force them back into the lead-lined box where she usually kept them.

'Seriously, what's the worst that could happen? If I made a move on you, you'd only have to say no.'

Her lips tightened even further. 'It would be awkward,' she squeezed out.

His snort drew the glance of the maître d'. 'Whereas this conversation is such a pleasure.'

'I don't think your sarcasm is warranted, Oliver.'

'Really? Your inference is that I would make some kind of fool of myself the very moment you're available.' Disbelief was wiggling itself a stronghold in his features. 'How new do you imagine I am to women, Audrey?'

He was so close to the truth now, she didn't dare speak. But that just gave him an empty stage to continue his monologue. And he was getting right into the part.

'I'm curious. Do you see me as pathetically desperate—' his whisper could have cut glass '—or is it just that you imagine yourself as so intensely desirable?'

Hurt speared straight down into that place where she kept the knowledge that she was the last sort of woman he'd want to be with. 'Stop it—'

But no. He was in flight.

'Maybe it wouldn't be that way at all. I'm considered quite a catch, you know. They even have a nickname for me. Could your crazy view of the world cope with the fact that I could make a move and you wouldn't be *able* to say no? Or want to?'

There was no way on this planet that he wouldn't see the sudden blanche of her face. The blood dropped from it as surely as if the sixty floors below them suddenly vaporised.

And *finally* he fell silent.

Stupid, blind, lug of a man.

Audrey stood and turned to stare at the dragonflies, her miserable arms curled protectively around her midsection where the intense ache was still resident. It was that or fling her hands up to her mortified face. Beyond the glass, the other diners carried on, oblivious to the agony swelling up to press with such intent against her chest wall.

'Is that it?' Oliver murmured behind her after a mute eternity. 'Is that why you don't want to be here?'

Mortification twisted tighter in her throat. She raised a finger to trace the glass-battering of a particularly furious dragonfly wedged in the corner of the tank who hadn't yet given up on its dream of freedom. 'I'm sure you think it's hilarious.'

The carpet was too thick and too new to betray his movement, but she saw his reflection loom up behind her. Over her. He stopped just before they touched.

'I would never laugh at you,' he said, low and earnest. 'And I would never throw your feelings back in your face. No matter what they were.'

She tossed her hair back a little. Straightened a little more. She might be humiliated but she would not crawl. 'No. I'm sure you've had prior experience with the inconvenient attachment of women.'

That was what made the whole thing so intensely humiliating. That she was just one of dozens—maybe hundreds—to fall for the Harmer allure.

'I care for you, Audrey.'

...*but*...

It had to be only a breath away. 'Oh, please. Save it for someone who doesn't know you so well.'

The soberness in his voice increased. 'I *do* care for you.'

'Not enough to come to my husband's funeral.' She spun. Faced him. 'Not enough to be there for your *friend* in the hardest week of her life when she was lost and overwhelmed and so bloody confused.' She reached for her handbag on the empty seat at the end of the table. 'Forgive me for suspecting that our compassion-meters aren't equally calibrated.'

With a deft swing, she had the handbag and all its contents over her shoulder and she turned toward the restaurant's exit. Remaining courses, be damned.

'Audrey—' His heavy hand curled around her upper arm. 'Stop.'

She did, but only because she'd made quite enough of a scene for one lifetime. And this was going to be the last memory of her he had; she didn't want it to be hysterical.

'I think I should explain—'

'You don't owe me an explanation, Oliver. That's what makes this whole situation so ridiculous. You owe me nothing.'

He wasn't hers to have expectations of. He wasn't even her husband's friend any more. He was just an acquaintance. A circumstantial friend.

At best.

'I wanted to be there, Audrey. For you. But I knew what would have happened if I'd flown in.' He took her hands in his and held them gently between them. 'You and I would have ended up somewhere quiet, nursing a generous drink and a bunch of stories long after everyone else had gone home, and you would have been exhausted and strung out and heartbroken.' She dipped her head and he had to duck his to keep up eye contact. 'And seeing that would have broken my heart. I would have taken you into my arms to give you support and make all the pain just vanish—' he took a deep breath '—and we would have ended up in bed.'

Her eyes shot back up. 'That wouldn't have happened—'

His hands twisted more firmly around hers, but not to hold her close. He used the leverage to push her gently away from him. 'It would have happened because I'm a heartbeat and some sorely tested willpower from doing it right now. I *want* you in my arms, Audrey. I *want* you in my bed. And it has nothing to do with Blake being gone because I've wanted the same thing each Christmas for the last five years.'

Every muscle in her body tensed up and he knew it.

Amazing, excruciating seconds passed.

'But that's not who we are,' he went on. 'I know that. Reducing what we have to the lowest common denominator might be physically rewarding but it's not what our... *thing*...is worth. And so what we're left with is this awkward...awareness.'

Awareness. So he felt it, too. But it wasn't just awkward, it was awful. Because she suddenly got the sense that it made Oliver as uncomfortable as it made her. Not expressing it, just...feeling it.

'I value your friendship, Audrey. I value your opinion and your perception and your judgement. I get excited coming up here in the elevator because I know I'm going to be seeing you and spending a day with you picking through your brilliant mind. The only day I get all year. I'm not about to screw that up by hitting on you.'

*Oh.* A small part of her sagged. But was it relief or disappointment? 'I'm so sorry.'

'Why?'

The blood must have returned to her face if she could still blush. 'Because it's such a cliché.'

'It's flattering. The fact that a woman I value so highly finds things in me to value in return is...validating. Thank you.'

'Don't thank me.' That was just a little bit too close to patronising.

'Okay. I'll just be silently smug about it instead.'

The fact that she could still laugh, despite everything… Yet, sure enough, the sound chuffed out of her. 'That seems more like you.'

They stood, nothing between them but air. And an emotional gulf as wide as the harbour.

'So now what?'

He considered her and then shook his seriousness free. 'Now we move on to the third course.'

# CHAPTER SIX

*Pineapple, hops, green tomato served in Brazil-nut-coated clusters*

DID THE EARTH lurch on its axis between courses for the rest of Qīngtíng's chic clientele? None of them looked overly perturbed. Maybe this building was constructed to withstand earth tremors.

Because Oliver's entire existence had just shifted.

The two of them retreated to silence and polite smiles as a stack of curious, bite-size parcels were placed before them and the waiter announced in his accented English, 'Pineapple and green tomato clusters coated in Brazil nut.'

The parcels might have been small but he and Audrey each took their time first testing and then consuming the tart morsels. Buying time. Really necessary time. Because the last thing he felt like doing was eating.

He'd come *this* close.

He almost touched her, back then when she'd turned her blanched face away from him with such dismay. He almost pulled her back into his chest and breathed down onto her hair that none of it mattered. Nothing that had gone before had any relevance.

Their slate started today, blank and full of potential.

But that wasn't just embarrassment on her face. That

was dread. She didn't *want* to be feeling any kind of attraction to him.

She didn't deserve his anger. He'd reacted automatically to the suggestion that he *was* as pitiful as he'd secretly feared when it came to her, but it wasn't Audrey's fault she'd pegged him so accurately. His anger was more appropriate directed at himself. *He* was the one who couldn't get another man's wife out of his head. *He* was the one who found himself incapable of being with a beautiful woman, now, and not wanting to peel back the layers to see the person inside. And *he* was the one who was invariably disappointed with what he found there, because they all paled by comparison.

Audrey was the best woman—the best human being— he knew. And he knew some pretty amazing people. But she was the shining star atop his Christmas tree of admired friends, just as glittering and just as out of reach.

And right up until a few minutes ago he'd believed she was safe territory. Because right up until a few minutes ago he had no idea that she was in any way into him. He'd grown so used to not acting on all the inappropriate feelings he harboured.

What the hell did he *do* in a world where Audrey Devaney was both single and into him?

'What happened with you and Blake?' she suddenly asked, cutting straight through his pity party. Her eyes were enormous, shimmering with compassion and curiosity. And something else... An edge of trepidation.

No. Not a conversation he could have with her. What would it achieve now that Blake was dead? 'We just... grew apart.'

Two pretty lines appeared between her brows. 'I don't understand why he didn't say something. Or suggest that I stop coming. For so long. That seems unlike him.'

'You'd expect him to force you to declare your allegiance?'

She picked her way, visibly, through a range of choices. 'He knew why I came here. He would have told me if it was no longer necessary.'

*Necessary.* The bubble of latent hope lost half of its air. The idea that she'd only been coming each year to please her husband bit deep. Attraction or no attraction.

'There must have been something,' she urged. 'An incident? Angry words?'

'Audrey, leave it alone. What does it matter now that he's gone?'

She leaned forward, over the nutty crumbs of the decimated parcels. 'I never did understand why you were friends in the first place. You're so different from Blake.'

'Opposites attract?' That would certainly explain his still-simmering need to absorb Audrey into his very skin. Too bad that was going to go insatiate. 'We weren't so different.' At least not at the beginning.

But, those all-seeing eyes latched onto the mystery and weren't about to let go. 'He did a lot of things that you generally disagreed with,' she puzzled. 'I'm trying to imagine what it would have taken to drive you away from him.'

Her unconscious solidarity warmed him right down to the place that had just been so cold. 'What makes you think it wasn't something *I* did?'

Her lips twisted, wryly. 'I knew my husband, Oliver. Warts and all.'

And that was about the widest opening he was ever going to get. 'Why did you marry him?'

The curiosity changed focus. 'Why do people usually marry?'

'For love,' he shot back. Not that he'd know what that looked like. 'Did you love him?'

And could she hear how much he was hoping the answer was 'no'?

'Marriage means different things to different people.'

Nice hedge. 'So what does it mean to you?'

She hesitated. 'I don't subscribe to the whole "lightning bolt across the crowded room" thing.'

It was true. There'd been no lightning bolt when she walked into the bar that first day. But when she'd first pinned him with her intellect and locked those big eyes on him just minutes later, he'd had to curl his fingers under the edge of the bar to keep from lurching backwards at the slam of *something* that came off her. Whatever the hell it was.

A big, blazing ball of slow burn.

'You don't aspire to that?' he dug.

'The great romantic passion? No.' A little colour appeared on her jaw. 'It hasn't been my experience. I value compatibility, shared interests, common goals, mutual respect, trust. Those are things that make a marriage.'

A hollow one, surely. Although how would he know? No personal experience to reference and a crap example in his parents' marriage, which barely deserved the title—just a woman living in the purgatory of knowing her husband didn't love her.

He risked a slight probe. 'Did Blake agree with that?'

She brought her focus back to him. 'I… Yes. We were quite sympathetic on a lot of things.'

Well, there was one area in particular that old Blake was definitely *un*sympathetic with Audrey.

*Fidelity.*

'You never looked at someone else and wondered what it might be like?' He had to know.

Her eyes grew wary. 'What *what* might be like?'

'To be with them. Did you never feel the pull of attraction to someone other than Blake and wonder about a relationship that started with good, old-fashioned lust?'

'You're assuming that *wanting* and *taking* are connected. It comes back to that mutual trust and respect. I just wouldn't do that to my partner. I couldn't.' Her eyes narrowed. 'I thought you, of all people, would understand that.'

A cold stone formed in his gut. *Of all people...* 'You're talking about my father?' They'd never discussed his father and so he knew whatever she knew had come from Blake. The irony of that...

'Was he very bad?'

He took a deep breath. But if sharing something with her, especially something this personal, was the only intimacy he was going to get from Audrey Devaney, he'd embrace it. 'Very.'

'How did you know what he was doing?'

'Everyone knew.'

'Including your mother?'

'She pretended not to.' For her son's sake. And maybe for her own.

'Did she not care?'

His stomach tightened at the memory of the sobbing he wasn't supposed to have heard when she thought he was asleep. His jaw tightened. 'She cared.'

'Why did she stay?'

The sigh wracked his body. 'My father was incapable of fidelity but he didn't drink, he was never violent, he remembered birthdays and he had steady employment. He was, in all other ways, a pretty reasonable father.'

If you didn't count a little thing called integrity.

Part of Oliver's own attraction to Audrey had always been her values. This was not a woman who would ever have knowingly done wrong by the man she shared vows with. Just a shame Blake hadn't returned the favour.

'So she chose to stay.' And that had been a green light in his father's eyes. The ultimate hall pass.

'Maybe she didn't think she could do better?'

'Than a man who was ruthlessly unfaithful—surely no one would think that?' It hit him then how freely he was having this discussion. After so many years of bleeding the feelings out in increments.

She shook her head. 'I don't know that you'll ever be able to relate. Because of who you are. Successful and charming and handsome. It's not that easy for everyone else.'

His heart swelled that she thought him handsome enough to say it aloud. 'You think I don't have my demons?'

She stared at him. 'I'm sure you do. But doubting your worth is not one of them.'

She wasn't wrong. His ego had been described by the media as 'robust' and in the boardroom as 'unspeakable'.

'And can you, Audrey? Relate?'

She stared out across the harbour to the towering giants on the other side. But her head nodded, just slightly. 'When I got to upper school I'd gone from being the tubby, smart girl to the plain, smart girl. I didn't mind that so much as long as it also came with "smart" because that was my identity, that was where I got my self-worth from. Academic excellence.'

'I wish I'd known you then.'

Her laugh grated. 'Oh, no… The beautiful people and I didn't move in the same hemisphere. You would never have even seen me then.'

'That's a big assumption to make.' And kind of judgemental. Which wasn't like her at all.

She leaned forwards. 'For the first two years of high school boys didn't want to know me. I was invisible and I just got on with things, under the radar. And then one day I got…discovered. And that was the end of my cruise through school.'

'What do you mean "discovered"?'

'The same way species are discovered even though they've been there for centuries. I didn't change my hair or get a makeover or tutor the captain of the football team. It wasn't like the movies. One day I was invisible and the next—' she shrugged '—there I was.'

'In a good way?'

She took a healthy swallow of her wine. 'No. Not for me.'

The pain at the back of her eyes troubled him. 'What happened?'

'Nothing. At first. They just watched me, wherever I went. Like they weren't sure how to engage with me.'

*They*...like a pack.

'One of them asked me out to a movie once. Michael Hellier. I didn't know how to say no kindly so I said yes and it was all over the school in minutes. They hunted me down, then, the girls from that group, and they slammed me against the bathroom wall and told me I was fishing outside of my swamp.' She lifted her eyes. 'But he'd asked me, I couldn't just not turn up. So I went. I don't even remember what film we saw because all I could think about the entire time I was with him was those girls. I convinced myself they were spying from the back row. I barely spoke to him and I didn't even take off my coat even though I was sweating like crazy under it, and when he tried to put his arm around me I literally froze. I sat there, totally rigid for the entire movie, and the moment the credits rolled I stammered out my thanks and I ran out of the cinema.'

Oliver sat silently, the whole, miserable story playing out in his mind, his anger bubbling up and up as it proceeded.

She turned more fully towards him, eyes blazing. 'I enjoyed it, Oliver. The attention of those boys. I enjoyed that none of them quite knew how to deal with me. I enjoyed being a puzzle in their eyes and I enjoyed how it made me feel. The shift in power. It felt like vindication forevery tease I'd endured as a kid. As if *"See! I am worthy."* I liked being visible. And I liked being sought after. I liked how fast my heart beat when I was near him because he was interested in me. And I totally played up to it.

'But I earned what happened to me.' She sighed. 'And I earned every cruel nickname they gave me after that. I tried to play a game I wasn't equipped for and I lost. I never made that mistake again. I never *reached* like that again. And after a while that starts to feel really normal. And so maybe something like that happened to your mother—'

God, he'd totally forgotten they'd been talking about Marlene Harmer.

'—something that taught her not to overreach.'

Or hope? Or expect more from people?

Or feel, maybe?

He asked the first thing that came to him. The thing he'd always, secretly, wanted to know. 'Is that why you chose Blake that day in the bar? Because some jerks in school taught you not to aim higher?'

The words hung, unanswered, between them. It was the first time either of them had ever acknowledged what had happened that night. How actively she'd focused her attention on Blake rather than on him. Almost to the point of rudeness.

And also hovering out there, in bright neon, was his presumption that Blake was somehow *less*. But deep down he knew that to be true—at least when it came to Audrey.

Audrey was never meant to be Blake's.

Not in a just world.

Indecision swam across her gaze, and he watched her trying to decide what was safe to reveal. When she did speak it was painfully flat and her eyes drifted slightly to his left. 'Blake was within reach.'

Low-hanging fruit.

Oliver flopped back against the rear of his sofa, totally lost for words, understanding, just a little bit, what Audrey had just said about vindication. He'd always wondered what drew Audrey to Blake instead of him that day, but such thoughts were arrogant and unkind given Blake was supposedly his best friend. So he'd swallowed them. Buried the question mark way down deep.

And now he had his answer.

An absurd kind of hope—totally at odds to the conversation they were having—washed through him.

Audrey didn't pick Blake because she deemed him the better man...

He was just the *safer* man.

Just like that, a whole side of her unfolded like spreading petals revealing an aspect to her he'd never suspected.

'It kills me to think that my mother would have harboured those kinds of feelings about herself and that my father would have reinforced them...'

Did she realise that when he said 'my mother' he really meant Audrey? And instead of his father, he meant himself? To imagine this extraordinary woman sitting in that bar all those years ago, smiling and chatting and sipping her drink and all the while going through a mental process that ended in her deciding she wasn't worthy—

*She!* The finest of women.

It killed him.

'You know her best,' Audrey murmured. 'I'm just hypothesising how she might have allowed that to happen. Everyone has a different story.'

Her furious back-pedalling made sense to him now. She'd exposed herself and so she was retreating to safer ground. But no, he wasn't about to let her do that. Not when he'd finally made some headway into knowing her.

Really knowing her.

He reached forward and took her hand. 'I wish I could impress upon her just how amazing a woman she is.'

She swallowed twice before answering. 'You could just tell her.'

'Do you think she'd believe me?' His thumb traced the shape of her palm. 'Or would she look for the angle?'

Hints of alarm etched across her expression. 'If you say it often enough eventually she'll have to believe you.'

Was it that simple? Could simple reinforcement undo the lessons—the experience—of years?

He released his breath slowly and silently. 'I would have seen you, Audrey. I give you my word.'

Because *she* was special, though, not because he was, particularly.

She tipped her head back towards the sofa-top. 'I could have done with a champion.'

Chivalrous wasn't exactly what he was feeling now, but he absolutely would have defended her against those who would have caused her this hurt. Who would have changed her essence.

He would have taken on half the school for her.

'And I could have done with your strength. And your maturity.'

She smiled, gently slipped her hand out from his and sat back against her seat. 'Really? Were you a wild child?'

Ah. Back to safety. Any topic other than her.

But he let her go, incredibly encouraged now that he'd picked up the key to getting inside her. Because the beautiful thing about keys was that you could use them as and when required. And in between you tucked them away somewhere safe.

This one he tucked away in a pocket deep inside his chest and he let her have the breathing space she obviously needed.

'Oh, the stories I could tell.'

'Go ahead.' She settled into her seat and seemed to have totally forgotten that less than half an hour ago she was heading for the door. 'We've still got five courses.'

Yep. That was what he had. Five courses and the rest of the day to make sure Audrey Devaney didn't disappear from his life forever.

# CHAPTER SEVEN

*Pomegranate, blood orange and Campari*

How was it possible that she'd just revealed more about herself in a few minutes to Oliver than she had in her entire marriage to her husband? Blake was all about the now; he lived for the moment, or planned for the future. But he spent no time looking back and he didn't ever show a particular interest in her past beyond what it meant for his present. They talked—a lot—and they shared ideas and grand schemes and they got excited about some and disappointed about others but it was never remotely personal.

She'd certainly never told him about those awful few months at school. He wouldn't have understood.

But if ever there was a man who should have not understood, he was sitting across from her today. Oliver with his comfortable background, his top-end schooling and his voted-most-likely-to-succeed status. Oliver *was* those boys from her past. He would have dated those girls that had slammed her up against the bathroom wall. He probably had!

He shouldn't have been able to empathise at all.

Yet he did. And it was genuine.

'Pomegranate, blood orange and Campari sorbet,' the maître d' announced, appearing at the side of their table with staff wielding another dish. In perfect synch, they positioned a fan of frosted antique tablespoons each packed with crushed ice and a ball of sorbet neatly balanced on the head of the spoon. They looked just like Christmas baubles sitting in snow.

'Thank you,' Audrey murmured, smiling as they left, bowing. After they'd gone, she added, 'They're very deferential to you, Oliver.'

'The quality of service is one of the things Qīngtíng is famous for.'

Mmm, still… 'They bow extra low to you.'

'I spend a fortune with them whenever I'm in Hong Kong.'

Suddenly the thought that he might come here with other people—maybe with other women—grew and flashed green in her mind. This was *their* place. It didn't exist when they weren't here, surely?

'Tell me about your year,' she blurted, to force the uncomfortable idea off her tongue before thought became voice. 'Did you ever hear from Tiffany?'

His lips twisted. 'She married someone else by Valentine's.'

'No! So fast? That's terrible.'

'He adores her and doesn't mind the lack of intelligent conversation. And she has more money than she can spend and a secure future. It was a good match.'

'Better than you?'

'Infinitely.'

'Why were you with her, Oliver? If she wasn't all that bright?'

His eyes shadowed and he busied himself with the sorbet. But he didn't change the subject and eventually he lifted his head to meet her eyes again. The faintest sheen dotted his tan forehead.

'Tiffany was engaging in her own way. I found her complete disregard for social convention refreshing. Besides,

I get my intelligent conversation elsewhere so I didn't feel the lack.'

'You were going to *marry* her, Oliver. Grow old with her, maybe father her children. And you didn't look to her for meaningful conversation?'

His lips thinned. 'Intellect isn't everything.'

No. Everyone had different strengths. She knew that better than most. Yet...

'Oliver. This is *you* we're talking about. You would have wasted away without a mental match in life.'

'What if I couldn't find a match?'

She practically snorted her pomegranate ice. 'That's a big call, isn't it? To assume that no woman could be your intellectual match.'

His eyes blazed. 'Not mine, Audrey. *Yours.*'

Her antique spoon clattered back onto its saucer.

But he didn't shy away from her startled gaze. 'You set a high bar, intellectually. Diversity of knowledge, your wit, your life experience. That's hard to equal.'

'Wh...' What was she supposed to say to that? 'Why would you *try* to match it?'

He leaned forwards, leading with his hazel eyes. 'Because you're the woman against which I measure all others, intellectually. You're my gauge of what's possible.'

'Me?' Her squeak was hardly the poster child for mental brilliance.

'And I haven't found anyone like you, yet.' He studied her as she squirmed. 'That makes you uncomfortable?'

'Yes!'

'Because you don't agree with my assessment of your smarts or because you don't want to be my bar?'

Her heart thundered so hard at the back of her throat she thought he might hear it pulsing below her words. 'Because pedestals are wobbly at the best of times.'

'Or is it just knowing that I consider us a perfect intellectual match that makes you nervous?'

If he said *intellectual* one more time she would scream; it only served to remind her how not matched they were in other ways.

She took a long breath. 'I'm flattered that you think so.' But only because of how highly she esteemed his mind. But then she saw how incredibly *un*-uncomfortable he looked. The devil lurked behind that sparkle in his eyes.

Oh.

'You're teasing me.'

'Hand on heart.' His big fist followed suit and he shook his head. 'But I knew your modesty wouldn't allow you to believe it.'

'You must meet some extraordinary people.'

'None who I'd want to spend an entire day just talking to.'

She stared, crippled by the monument of that. 'No pressure, then.'

Two diners looked around at Oliver's bark of laughter. 'Yeah, the next word out of your mouth better impress.'

She consciously coordinated the muscles necessary to breathe and then used the outward part of the breath to say, 'Euouae.'

Oliver blinked.

'It's a musical mnemonic to denote the sequence of tones in the Seculorum Amen.'

'See what I mean?' His smile broke out on one side of that handsome mouth. 'Who knows that?'

She blew out a long breath. 'It's also the longest word in the English language made up of only vowels.'

'Okay, now you're just showing off. Eat your sorbet.'

'Thank you, Oliver,' she said, as soon as her mind would work properly again. 'That's quite a compliment.'

'No, actually, it's a curse. I can't tell you how many dinners I've sat through waiting for something like Eweyouu—'

'Euouae.'

'—to casually come up.'

'Hopefully none of those meals were as long as this one, then.'

'I'm serious, Audrey; you've spoiled me for other women.'

And just like that she was speechless again. And her blood was back to its thundering.

*Intellectually*, she reminded herself. *Only in that one way.* Because the women Oliver Harmer chose had beauty and grace and breeding and desirability and experience and, Lord knew, more elasticity than she could ever aspire to.

'So, you just…lowered your bar?'

'I decided that I could get my fix of conversational stimulation every Christmas instead.'

'You're assuming that your wife would be happy for us still to meet each year. I'm not sure I would be if you were—' she nearly choked on the word '—mine.'

He shrugged. 'It wouldn't be negotiable.'

'Famous last words. What would happen when you were completely smitten with her and she turned her big violet eyes up to you and let them fill with tears and begged you not to go?'

'Really? Violet.'

'I'm sure she'd be exceptional.'

He gave her that point. 'I'd hand her a Kleenex and tell her I'd see her later that evening.'

'And if she let her robe fall open and seduced you into staying?'

His eyes darkened. 'Then I'd cancel the car and take the chopper to make up the lost time.'

'And if she threatened you with divorce?'

'Then I'd call my lawyer and let him deal with the weeping,' he huffed, eyes rolling. 'Do you imagine I'm so easily manipulated, Audrey?'

No. She couldn't imagine him falling for any of that.

'So what if the woman that loved you sat you down and stoically explained how much it hurt her that you got from someone else something she couldn't give you.'

His pupils enlarged and then the deepest of frowns surrounded them. 'God, Audrey…'

Had he never thought about what it might do to the woman 'lucky' enough to get him? She much preferred to think that a woman he chose would select door number four. The vaguely dignified option. Of course, the alternative would be to say nothing and just *ache* every year as December twentieth approached.

Yeah, that had worked really well for her.

He blew air from between tight lips and forked his fingers through his hair.

'You see my point?' she murmured.

'So you're basically dooming me to a bachelor's life forever, then? Because I've been looking, Audrey, and you're not out there.'

'I'm just saying you can't have Frankenstein's bride.'

He tipped his head.

'You don't want a regular woman with flaws and room for improvement. You want the intelligence of one woman, the courage of another, the serenity of a third. And you want it all wrapped up in a beautiful exterior.'

'She doesn't have to be beautiful.'

*Pfff.* 'Yes, she does, Oliver. You only date stunning women.' The Internet was full of pictures of him with his latest arm decoration.

'You think I'm that shallow?'

All right then… 'When was the last time you were seen in public with a plain, ordinary woman?' she challenged.

And he shot back, fast and sure. 'I have lunch with one every Christmas.'

The air whooshed out of her, audibly. But it wasn't indignation and she didn't flounce out. She sat as straight and dignified as she could and opened her mouth to say something as witty as he probably expected. But absolutely nothing came to her.

So she just closed it again.

He swore. 'Audrey, I'm sorry. I spoke carelessly. That was supposed to be a compliment.'

Because he deigned to lower himself long enough to eat in public with a less than beautiful woman? 'Your flattery could do with some refinement, then,' she squeezed out.

'You are so much more than the particular arrangement of your features. I see all the things you *are* when I look at you, not the things you *aren't*.'

Clumsy, but at least he wasn't patronising her with claims of inner beauty.

'Please, Audrey. You're the last person on this planet that I would want to hurt. Or that I'm fit to judge. My social circle tends to fill with beautiful stars on the rise. I don't date them for the pleasure of sitting there looking at them. I date them to see what else they have going for them.'

It wasn't all that inconceivable. She could well imagine the facility with which a stunning woman would find herself with access to the kind of people Oliver mixed with. Where else was he going to meet women? And she absolutely couldn't blame them for being drawn to him, once there. He was Oliver Harmer.

He took her hand across the table. 'It's really important to me that you don't think I'm that kind of man.'

And it wasn't as if he were giving her a news flash. She detached her hand from his under the pretence of wiping her mouth with her napkin and sighed. But she wasn't about to be a princess about this. She was a big girl.

'I wake up to myself every day, Oliver. I know where my virtues lie.' Or didn't.

'I would give every cent I have—' The greenish-brown of his eyes focused in hard but as he spoke he turned away, so that the words were an under-breath jumble. And something in his expression made her really want to know what came next.

'Every cent, what?'

'For you to recognise your strengths.'

Had even the kitchen staff stopped to listen? Every sound that wasn't Oliver's low voice seemed to have vanished. But something stopped her from letting his words fill her heart with helium.

'I don't need you to do this, Oliver.' In fact she really would rather he didn't. 'I don't care what you think of my appearance.'

'Of course you do. Because you're human and because I just reinforced all those jerks at your school with my stupid, careless words.' He stood and pulled her to her feet. '*I* care what you think of *my* appearance.'

It was such a ludicrous concept—not that he cared, but that there was any question about how good he looked— she actually laughed. Out loud. 'No, you don't.'

'I changed three times before coming here today.'

She looked him over, some of her pre-shock spirit returning. 'And this was your best effort?'

The lips that gaped at her then were stained slightly red with pomegranate ice and looked more than a little bit like they were flush from kissing. 'This is all brand-new gear!'

'Oh, you shopped too? Wow.' Her umbrage eased a bit more.

'And I didn't shave this morning because you once said you liked stubble. Four years ago.'

A reluctant laugh tumbled out of her. 'Oh, that's just sad, Oliver.' It didn't matter why he was demeaning himself to stave off her further embarrassment, she was just very grateful that he was. She peered up at him. 'I know what you're doing.'

'What am I doing?'

'You're lying. To make me feel better.'

His eyes narrowed as he towered over her. 'Is it working?'

'Yes, actually.' Purely based on the fact he cared enough to try. He'd meant what he said but he hadn't meant it to be hurtful.

He took half a step closer. 'Great then.'

'Besides, you always look good. You don't have to try.'

'Small mercy. There are plenty more ways that I feel deficient around you, Audrey.'

The wealthiest and most successful man she knew? 'Like how?'

Indecision carved that handsome face. 'I live in fear that I'll glance up suddenly and catch you looking at me with the kind of patient, vacant tolerance I give most of my dates.'

'You think I'm humouring you?'

His shrug only lifted one big shoulder. 'You only came here at all because of Blake. Maybe it's all Christmas charity.'

The thought that she'd caused someone to question themselves the way she had—even someone as profusely confident as Oliver—made her squirm. Though she knew the ramifications of correcting him were steep.

'I'm still here, aren't I?'

He knuckled a loose piece of her hair more securely behind her ear. 'Ah, but you came to say goodbye.'

'I did,' she breathed. That was totally her plan when she walked in. Until something had changed without her consent. 'So why haven't I?'

His eyes glittered and his hand turned palm side up and

curled around her cheek. 'Something else I'd give my fortune to know.'

A steam train thundered through her brain. 'You're rapidly running out of fortunes.'

'Benefit of a double-A credit rating.' His thumb crept across to trace the shape of her bottom lip. 'I can get more.'

'What are you doing?' she whispered, and he knew exactly when to drop the game.

'Everything I can before you tell me to stop.'

She absolutely should. They were in a public place and this was *'The Hammer'*, notorious player and corporate scourge of Asia. And more to the point, this was Oliver. She had no business letting him this close, no matter how much the furthest corner of her soul tried to tell her differently.

It didn't matter that she was no longer anyone's wife. It didn't matter that he was the one controlling the lazy drag of his fingers and therefore any resulting public exposure. Those things only made it more dangerous. More ill advised.

But as his hazel eyes blazed down on her and his big, smooth thumb pressed against the flesh of her lips she struggled to remember any of those things.

And her mouth opened.

# CHAPTER EIGHT

*Baked scallops, smoked eel with capsicum salsa and a
Parmesan and dill crust.*

'Stop.'

She wasn't inviting him in. She was locking him out.
Of course she was. This was Audrey.

Oliver drew his hands back into his own personal space
and stepped away from her, more towards the wall-that-
would-be-a-window. The soothing, ancient presence of the
mountains far behind Victoria Harbour anchored him and
stopped his heart from beating clear through his chest and
then through all that glass into the open air of the South
China Sea.

'Shorter than I'd hoped,' he murmured at the vast open
space. Yet so much further than he'd ever imagined he'd get.

'We're in a public restaurant, Oliver.'

'I have a suite just upstairs.' As if that were really what
stopped her.

But she ignored the underlying meaning. Again, because
she was Audrey. The woman had more class than he could
ever hope to aspire to.

'I thought we were on the top floor?' she said, smooth-
ing her skirt and keeping the conversation firmly off what
had just happened. All that…touching.

'The top public floor. There's a penthouse.' Technically part of the sixtieth floor but a half-dozen metres higher.

'And you have it?'

He turned and faced her. And the music. 'It came with the restaurant.'

Her brows dipped over slightly glassy eyes. He loved that he'd made them that way. But then they cleared and those fine brows lifted further than he imagined they could go. 'You *bought* the restaurant?'

'I did.'

She shook her head. 'What's the matter? No good restaurants closer to Shanghai?'

'I like this one.'

And Qīngtíng had the added advantage of being saturated in echoes of his time together with Audrey. And when she didn't come last year he began to believe that might be all he'd ever have of her.

Memories.

'Clearly.' And then her innate curiosity got the better of her. 'What did it cost?'

God, he adored her. So classy and yet so inappropriate at the same time. Absolutely no respect for social niceties. But he wasn't ready to put a price tag on his desperation just yet. Bad enough that his accountant knew.

'More than you can imagine. It wasn't on the market.' He'd just kept offering them more until they caved.

Understanding filled her eyes. 'That's why you seemed so familiar with the dragonfly keeper. And why they bow so low for you.' And why he got to call the chef *Gerard*. 'You're their boss.'

'They treat everyone that well,' he defended. Badly.

'Why did you buy it?'

Uh…no. Not something he was going to admit to the woman who'd made it clear she wasn't after anything more with him. In words and, just moments ago, in deed.

He cleared his throat. 'It's a fantastic investment. The return is enormous.' As much an unexpected bonus as the big, luxurious, lonely suite right above their heads. 'Do you want to see it?'

She turned her confusion to him.

'The penthouse. It's pretty spectacular.'

'Is it...? Are you...?' She took a deep breath. 'Will you be sleeping there tonight?'

Was that her subtle way of asking whether there was a bed up there? 'You're safe with me, Audrey.'

Heat flared at her jaw. 'I know.'

Though, hadn't he been the one to instigate the touch-a-thon just now? 'It's so much more than a bedroom. It's like a small house perched atop this steel mountain.' She didn't have a prayer of hiding the spark of interest. So he went for the kill shot. 'Every window gives you a different view of Hong Kong.'

She was inordinately fond of this city, he knew. In fact, pretty much anything oriental. It made him wonder what she'd thought of Shanghai; if she'd liked it as much as he did.

And why, exactly, was that important...?

Indecision wracked her face. She wanted to see it, but she didn't want to be alone with him away from the security of a restaurant full of unwitting chaperones. So who did she trust less—him or herself?

Her eyes flicked to her left as two restaurant staff approached from the direction of the beautifully disguised kitchens and placed their next dish on the table.

'Oh, great!'

Audrey hadn't been quite that animated about the arrival of the previous dishes. But she certainly rushed back to her seat with enthusiasm now. Oliver half smiled and followed her.

'Scallops and smoked eel swimming in a sea of capsicum with a Parmesan and dill crust,' Ming-húa announced before departing. Each dish composed of an enormous white shell in which three tender scallop and eel pairs sat, awash, in a red liquid salsa. A two-pronged splade balanced across each one.

'Did Blake burn you financially?' Audrey asked, breathless, as she tucked into her scallops.

It was absolutely the last thing he expected her to say, although retreating behind the memory of her departed husband shouldn't have surprised him.

'No. Why?'

'I figured money would have to be the only thing big enough to drive a wedge between the two of you.'

Oliver moderated a deep breath. She wasn't going to let this go. 'Look, Audrey…Blake and I were friends for a long time and people change in that time. Values change. The more time we spent apart, the less we had in common.'

Except for Audrey. She was their constant.

'I just don't understand why he would have kept it a secret, unless it was a big deal of some kind.'

Even in absentia, he was still lying to cover his old friend's ass. But it was more than that. Hadn't she just shared the misery of her childhood, all those issues with self-worth? What would it do to her to learn her husband was a serial adulterer?

The burning need to protect her surged through him. 'Let it go, Audrey.'

But something was clearly troubling her. She was eating the scallop as though it were toast. Biting, chewing and swallowing with barely any attention on the succulent food. 'What values?'

He faked misunderstanding.

'You said that values changed with time. What values changed between the two of you, if it wasn't about business?'

'Audrey—'

'Please, Oliver. I need to know. Was it your values?'

'Why do you need to know?'

She eyed him as she slipped the last succulent morsel between her lips. 'Because a few years before he died, he changed. And I want to know if it's connected.'

Dread pooled in his belly. 'Changed how?'

'He just…' She frowned, trying to focus what was obviously a lot of thoughts all rushing her at once. 'He became…affectionate.'

The second surprise in his day. 'Affectionate?'

'He grew all touchy-feely. And he'd never done that before.'

'You got worried because he got *more* intimate with you?' Exactly what kind of a marriage had they had?

'It was just notable by its sudden presence.' She cleared her throat. 'And it escalated every November. Like clockwork.'

The weeks leading up to her annual pilgrimage to Hong Kong. Overcompensating for the fact that he was lining up to betray her in the most fundamental way possible, probably.

'So I thought…that is, I wondered…' She closed her eyes and took a long slow breath. 'I thought it might have been related to me coming here. That he was struggling with it.'

'But he was the one who encouraged you.'

'I know, that's the part I don't understand. But I knew he had problems with how I was with you when we were all together and so I thought maybe he believed—'

She snapped her mouth shut.

*How I was with you…* Oliver filed that one away for later dissection. 'He believed what?'

'That there was something going on.' She flushed. 'With us.'

There were no words. Oliver could only stare. She was

so very far off the mark and yet so excruciatingly close to the truth.

'But there wasn't,' he hedged.

'Blake didn't know that.' She threw her hands up. 'It's the only thing I can think of to explain it.'

*Is it really, Audrey?*

It wasn't until she spoke that he realised he had—aloud. 'What do you mean?'

Crap. 'I mean there could be dozens of other alternatives. Blake knew he could trust you with his life.'

That was what made his betrayal all the more vile.

'I thought, maybe he confronted you with it and, knowing how you felt about your father, you might have been insulted and the two of you might have fought…?'

Maybe that was what her subconscious wanted her to believe.

'He didn't confront me.' That much he could safely say. Blake was the confront*ee* not the confront*er*.

'Oh.' Those two appealing little forks appeared between her brows again. 'Okay.'

She was out of ideas. Oliver knew he could just change the subject and she'd go with that because that brilliant mind of hers was flirting around the edges but was determined not to see the possibility of truth. And who could blame her?

But would it eat at her forever?

She lifted the half-shell and used the splade to scoop up some of the rich, vibrant sauce. Her frown didn't dissipate even as she sipped at her dish.

No. She wasn't going to let her curiosity die with her husband. She was just going to let it fester and worsen her deeply suppressed self-doubt as only secrets could. But telling her the truth wouldn't achieve much better.

Except maybe bring it all out into the light where she could deal with it. Surely something like that lost some of its power when it was exposed to the light. Rather than poisoning as a fear. If Audrey knew nothing, he'd have been content to leave it that way but she knew enough that she would eventually work her way around to the truth or, if not that, then her subconscious would whisper cruelly in her ears forever. Or she'd hear it from someone else instead of in the protective company of a friend.

He studied her strong face and made his decision.

'It was guilt, Audrey.' The splade froze halfway to her mouth. 'If Blake changed then he was overcompensating because he knew what was going to happen the moment you left the country.'

Those enormous blue eyes grew. 'What do you mean?'

He took a deep breath and trashed the memory of a dead man.

'Your husband had affairs, Audrey. Lots of them. Every year while you were here with me.'

The effusive apologies of the staff for what was essentially her own mistake bought Audrey a few precious moments to get her act together. Immaculate girls in exotic Chinese silk dabbed and pawed at the ruined linen of her outfit where the splade, the shell and its entire remnant contents had tumbled out of her deadened fingers.

Oliver watched her with concern through the chaos and all the bodies.

She'd never had so many hands on her breasts and thighs at one time. How ironic to consider that in the same moment as discovering that her husband—who'd barely troubled himself to pay more than businesslike attention to the private parts of her body—was apparently sleeping all around town the moment she left the country.

Betrayal stung, heated and raw in that place behind her heart she never let anyone go.

And tears stung just as angry in her eyes.

'Ming-húa—' Oliver barked and then spoke quietly to the maître d', who then rattled a fast command to his staff who, in turn, scattered on individual errands. One left a clean towel with Audrey but it wasn't going to do much against the red stain that spread like a chest-wound down her cream front.

'Come on,' Oliver said, pulling her to her feet. 'You can change upstairs.'

Code for *I'm taking you somewhere you can have your meltdown in private.*

She let him pull her towards the exit, his hand hot and secure around her ice-cold one. But as they got to the elevators he led her, instead, up a carpeted circular staircase, which opened discreetly onto one side of the public restaurant lobby.

At the top of the stairs, the furnishings changed slightly to the polished floor and neutral décor so popular in this part of China. It actually felt quite welcoming since her home in Australia was much the same. Executive beige. Blake's taste, not hers. All very stylish but totally without soul.

Like their marriage.

Oliver swiped a keycard through the scanner and swung open a pair of big, dark doors into an amazing space.

The view shouldn't have stolen her gaze so immediately considering it was only a half-floor higher than the restaurant they'd spent all afternoon in, but the penthouse sat squarely on the top of the building and its windows wrapped around three-hundred-and-sixty degrees of amazing view. Some of it was the much taller buildings around them and the patches of mountainside in between, but the majority was the towering chrome and glass forest that was the buildings of Central Hong Kong and, across the harbour, Kowloon.

It didn't matter that the living area wasn't large because it had the most spectacular back yard she'd ever seen.

Pity she was in no mood to enjoy it.

'Tell me,' she gritted the moment the door closed behind her.

But Oliver waited until he'd removed her dripping jacket and folded it on the non-porous safety of the slate bench top in the open-plan kitchen. Short of removing her blouse and skirt, too, there wasn't much else he could do to clean her up.

Audrey folded her arms across her damp front and walked to the enormous window to just…stare.

'He called them his Christmas bonus.' Oliver sighed behind her.

Pain lanced through her. That was just crass enough for Blake, too. 'Who were they? Where did he find them?'

'I don't know, Audrey.'

'How long have you known? The whole three years?'

'The first year I thought maybe he'd grow out of it. But when he did it again the following year, I realised it wasn't a one-off. So I confronted him about it.'

She squeezed her hands around her elbows. 'So…five years in total? Also known as *our whole marriage*?'

Her voice shook on that and she saw him behind her, reflected in the glass of the balcony, his head bowed. The most defeated she'd ever seen him.

'I'm so sorry, Audrey. You don't deserve this.'

'Why didn't you tell me sooner?' she whispered.

'Because I knew how much it would hurt you.'

She spun. 'You preferred to leave me in a marriage where I was being made a fool of?'

'I couldn't be sure you didn't know.'

She couldn't prevent the rise in her voice. 'You thought I might *know* and *stay*?'

Like his mother? Was that what his upbringing taught him?

'I couldn't be sure,' he repeated. 'It's not an easy subject to raise.'

Which would explain why half their day had gone by before he elected to mention it.

'Is *this* why you didn't come to his funeral?'

'I've explained why—'

'Right. In case you couldn't keep your hands off me.' She snorted. 'I didn't actually believe you about that.' The hurt she was feeling had to go somewhere, and Oliver was right there.

'Well, you should, because I meant every word. Why do you think I sent your favourite flowers and not his? I wanted to be there for *you*.'

'Just a shame that Blake didn't share your enthusiasm for me or he may not have felt the need to stray.'

Ugh. Even the word sounded so wretched. And even though her head knew that *Blake* was the one who'd been so sad and weak, it didn't stop her from feeling like the pathetic one.

'So you and he…' Oliver risked.

She spun around. 'Did we have a rich and fulfilling sex life? Apparently not. I knew I didn't rock his world but I didn't realise I'd driven him to such desperate lengths.'

'It wasn't you, Audrey.'

'It was at least half me!'

He crossed to her, took her hands from around her ruined blouse and cupped them. 'It wasn't you at all.'

'Well, it wasn't Don bloody Juan. He seems to have had no problems in that regard.'

'I swear to you, Audrey, there was nothing you could have done differently.'

'How would you know? Did he—?' *Oh, God.* 'Did he talk to you about our sex life, or lack thereof?'

Yeah, that would be the final humiliation. Oliver could add *dud lay* to her mounting debit column.

'No. He did not. But he did talk quite freely about his other...encounters. Until I shut that down.'

She sunk onto an ottoman and buried her face in her hands. 'I feel like such a fool. How could I not have seen?'

'He didn't want you to see.'

'Then how could I not have guessed?' She shot back up onto her feet. 'We lived such separate lives but I was with him every day—surely I should have at least suspected?'

'Like I said, you look for the best in people.'

'Not any more,' she vowed.

'Don't.' He crossed to stand in front of her. 'Don't let him change you. Your goodness is why people will judge him for this, not you.'

*People?* Her face came up. 'How many people know?'

He dropped his eyes to the carpet. 'A few. I gather he wasn't all that subtle.'

A sudden image of Blake with a buxom post-adolescent on each arm strolling through inner Sydney filled her mind and thickened her throat. Everything she wasn't. Young, stacked, lithesome and probably the kind of performer in bed that she could never hope to be.

And so public... Maybe he wanted to be caught? Wasn't that what the experts said about men who had affairs? And maybe she would have caught him out if she'd been paying the slightest bit of attention to her marriage.

Reality soaked in as the tears dried up. She'd set herself up for this the day she gave her work and her friends and her hobbies more importance than her marriage.

She straightened on a deep inward breath.

'Audrey...' Oliver warned, his voice low. 'I know what you're doing.'

She tossed back her hair. 'What am I doing?'

'You're tallying up the ways this is your fault.'

He knew her so well. How was that possible?

'Do I need to say it again?' he growled.

'Apparently you do.'

He stared at her, indecision scouring that handsome face. Then he stepped forward and took her hands again, squatting in front of her. 'Audrey Devaney, this was *not* your fault.'

He spoke extra-slowly to get through her hysteria.

'There was nothing in this world that you could have done to change this—' he tightened his hold on her hands so much she actually glanced down at his white knuckles '—short of changing gender.'

Her tear-ravaged eyes shot back up to his one more time. Utterly speechless. But then denial kicked in.

'No—'

'I think he'd known a really long time,' he went on, calmly. 'I think he knew when we were growing up, I think he knew when you guys first started dating and I think he knew when he walked down the aisle with you. But I also think he just couldn't be on the outside what he didn't feel on the inside. Not long term.'

'You're defending him?'

'I'm defending his right to be who he truly was. But, no, I'm not defending his actions. Cheating is cheating and he was hurting someone I care deeply about. That is why I ended my friendship with him.'

'And he knew that?'

'He got a very graphic farewell visit.'

'You were in Sydney? Why didn't you tell me?' Although the answer to that was ridiculously patent. To someone whose brain cells weren't in a jumbled pile. 'Sorry. Don't answer that.'

Just then the tiniest knock came at the big brown doors. Almost like a kitten scratching. Oliver crossed to it and pulled one open and one of the stunning staff from earlier drifted in. She held a neat fold of gorgeous blue silk, threaded through with silver.

'A change of clothes for you,' Oliver explained. 'Your suit will be laundered onsite and returned to you before you leave tonight.'

The girl smiled, revealing flawless, tiny teeth to go with the hourglass figure and hand-span waist, and nudged the clothes towards her. Audrey felt foolish being treated with such kid gloves, so she took the clothes, thanked the girl and turned to go find a bathroom.

'Second on the right,' Oliver called after her.

It was a matter of only minutes for her to strip out of her ruined business suit and into the dress that the girl had clearly picked up in the boutiques on street level. Three-quarter length, with the high collar and short sleeves typical of Chinese fashion and accentuating every curve. The depth of the blue was truly stunning and the threads of silver cast a glow that refracted up to include her face.

Which only served to highlight the tear-struck devastation there. As if things weren't bad enough.

She sagged down onto the broad bath edge and slumped, exhausted, against the cool of the tiled wall.

Blake's secret life certainly explained a lot. His at times enigmatic behaviour, which she'd chalked up to business tensions. His emotional detachment, never rude but always a few degrees…separated. And their lacklustre—and downright perfunctory—sex life.

Technically correct but lacking any real heart.

Turned out there was a very good reason for that.

And *she* wasn't *it*.

Her relief at that far eclipsed the shock of discovering her husband was gay. How sad that Blake hadn't ever managed to reconcile that part of his life. That he felt the need to lie to everyone around him even while it ate him up inside.

And how sad that she couldn't have been there for him in his struggle. Because she would have. Her feelings for him might not have been traditional or immense but they were genuine, even when she didn't always like the things he did. If he'd confided in her, she totally would have supported him. Even as she left him.

Because hiding inside a marriage was no way to be happy.

Audrey looked back up into the mirrors lining the far side of the bathroom and practically heard them whisper…

*Hypocrite.*

She'd held onto her fair share of secrets, too, within their marriage. Not quite as destructive as Blake's, but then again her secrets weren't quite as colossal as his.

She tilted her head slightly back in the direction of the living room. Towards Oliver.

*Not quite.*

Thanks to China and its quirks, Audrey knew exactly what she'd find under the bathroom sink. A small refrigerator loaded with bottles of water and, on the left, a stack of dampened, refrigerated towels. Manna during Hong Kong's steamy wet season. Stocked just because during the dry. A lifesaver now.

She pressed the topmost wet towel to her flushed face, trying to restore some semblance of order.

'Audrey?' Oliver murmured through the door.

She opened it just a crack.

'I thought you might want this?' He squeezed her purse through to her.

'Thank you. Um…here…' She bundled up her skirt and blouse and passed the whole wad back through the gap. 'So she doesn't have to wait.'

As his fingers closed around the clothes they brushed against hers, static sparking in their wake. Except it couldn't be static because she was standing on tiles and the corridor was bamboo-floored. She curled her fingers back into her palm as she pulled it back into the bathroom.

Oliver murmured and was gone.

It took two more towels and some hasty repair work with the travel make-up from her purse until she felt vaguely presentable again. She combed through her chaos of hair, pulled the snug blue dress down the few inches it had ridden up with all her fussing and turned to the door.

Ready or not.

# CHAPTER NINE

*Ginger fingers with lemon spritzer*

'How are you doing?'

It took Oliver a moment to speak after she emerged and when he did there was a hint of tightness to his voice. Uncomfortable at the idea of picking up the conversation where they left off, perhaps, given how hysterical she'd been.

Well, that was over.

The beautiful hostess had departed with her things and so they were alone again, but Audrey wasn't about to resume their previous discussion. She ignored his question and wandered straight past him into a kitchen that looked as if it had been shipped direct from a magazine. And also as if it had never made so much as a cup of coffee. And why would it when the residences in this building were fully serviced by maids and room service?

'Why do you suppose they need two sinks?' she mused.

Excellent. Displacement conversation.

There were dual sinks on opposite sides of the kitchen. Neither of them overlooked the magnificent view, so they clearly weren't for standing at doing dishes.

Oliver moved up behind her. 'Maybe the wealthy entertain a lot? Need the catering facility?'

She turned. 'You say that like you're not one of them.'

'Entertaining is really not where I spend my money.'

'You entertain me every Christmas.'

'You're an exception to the rule.' He watched her as she trailed a finger along the granite bench tops, drifting slowly amongst all the polished surfaces. 'That dress looks—'

He struggled for words and she hoped whatever he was trying not to say wasn't *ridiculous*. Or *absurd*. Or *try hard*.

'—like it's part of your skin. It fits you perfectly.'

It shouldn't, given she was taller by a foot than the average Chinese delicacy. She glanced down at her legs where the dress stopped awkwardly halfway up her calves. 'I think it's supposed to be longer.'

'It doesn't matter. It looks right on you.'

She bowed in a parody of the cultural tradition and as she came up she saw the burst of dark intensity in his gaze. She swallowed with some difficulty. 'That's because you haven't seen me try to sit down in it, yet.'

But that wasn't nearly as difficult as she feared. The dress shifted and gave in all the right places as she sank down onto the edge of the expensive nine-seat sofa running around the far edges of the living space.

'Are we going to ignore it, Audrey?' Oliver said, still standing a few feet away.

*It.* The proverbial elephant in the room. 'I'm not sure there's much more to say.'

His eyes narrowed. 'Just like that? You've filed it away and dealt with it already?'

No, she'd filed it away *un*-dealt with. As was her wont. She smiled breezily. 'I really don't want to have to reapply my make-up a second time.'

Oliver stared down on her. 'It bothers you that little?'

Oh, where to begin answering that question? Her tight smile barely deserved the title. 'Many things about what he did will always bother me. It bothers me that I misread our marriage so much. It bothers me that he respected it little

enough to cheat in the first place. It bothers me that he respected *me* little enough to do it and be so public about it.'

'But not that it was with men?'

She stared. 'You said it yourself. It wasn't *me*. It wasn't
Audrey Devaney that he felt the need to stray from; it wasn't
*his wife* that he couldn't stomach. It was all of us. My whole
gender. There's no better or cleverer or funnier or sexier
woman that might have been more suitable than me. His
choice means my only lack was a Y chromosome.'

'You don't lack anything, Audrey.'

*Get real.*

She leaned forward. 'You know my school experience.
That led me to bury myself in study during university and
not long after graduating I met Blake.' And Oliver, but that
wasn't going to help make her point. 'So my entire sense of
who I am romantically—' she couldn't even bring herself
to *say* 'sexually' '—was from him.'

A man who was just going through the motions for ap-
pearances' sake.

'I thought it was *me*. I thought I was to blame for the
lack of passion in our marriage. That I didn't inspire it, that
I wasn't worth it.'

That she couldn't feel it.

She shuddered in a breath. 'All those tears you just wit-
nessed thirty minutes ago, all that devastation…? That was
because the only man I've ever been intimate with preferred other women to me. Because that's how much of a
dud I was in bed. But here I sit, just twenty minutes later,
tearless and comparatively whole. I'm not mourning my
marriage, I'm not cursing Blake's cheating, I'm not even
cursing him.' She lifted wretched eyes to his. 'What does
it say about me that my first reaction on hearing about all
those men was *relief*? Vindication. Because that meant it
wasn't *me*. That maybe I'm not broken.'

'I think it says you're human, Audrey. Which I know

won't please you. You're a perfectionist and you like things to be orderly.' He peered down on her. 'And you're certainly not broken.'

She shot to her feet. 'Words. How would you know? Maybe a hotter woman might have been able to satisfy him.'

Oliver smiled. 'Pretty sure it doesn't work like that.'

'My point is that Blake is still my only reference point. So, really, we know nothing. I could still be a dud.'

Jeez, with self-belief like that who needed enemies?

Oliver folded his arms and calmly watched her pace. 'You haven't been involved with anyone else since he died? It's been eighteen months.'

'I've been too busy shoring up my life,' she defended, instantly conscious that maybe it was just further evidence of her lameness. Shoring up her life and conveniently returning directly to type. Her barricaded-up, risk-averse type.

'Audrey, think. You're missing something obvious—'

'Apparently I've been missing it for years!' That her husband wasn't into women. She spun on him. 'And why the hell does this amuse you?'

'—*I'm* attracted to you.'

*Pfff.* 'You just think the dress is hot.'

Yet her pulse definitely spiked at his words. But, once again, words were cheap.

'I do think the dress is hot but she had a similar one on, too—' he nodded to the front door where the beautiful china doll had just departed '—and I wasn't attracted to her. And you weren't wearing it earlier and I was definitely attracted to you then.'

'You're Oliver—*The Hammer*—Harmer. You'd be attracted to anyone.'

His fists curled that little bit tighter. 'You're going to need to find one slur and stick to it, Audrey. Either I'm guilty of swimming too exclusively down the beautiful end of the gene pool or I'll do anything in a skirt. Which is it?'

'I didn't say you couldn't slum it from time to time.'

That actually seemed to make him mad. For the first time today. 'I think you'd say anything to win an argument.'

Yep. He absolutely had her number there.

Well… Whatever. 'You being attracted to me is a comment on your general randyness not on my abilities—' or otherwise, a little, inner voice whispered '—in the sack.'

He laughed but it no longer sounded amused. 'Careful, Audrey. That sounds an awful lot like a challenge.' He stepped closer.

She tossed her head. 'How like you to read it that way.'

'Why are you so angry at me?'

'Because you're here,' she yelled. 'And because you kept this from me for so long. And because you're—'

*Part of the bloody problem.*

If not for the extraordinary chemistry she'd always felt around Oliver she might never have noticed it missing from her marriage. But she forced those words back into her throat before they spilled out, and let the tension out on a frustrated grunt instead.

'Because I'm what?'

'You're pushing me.'

'I'm trying to support you. I'm listening. And letting you vent. How is that pushing?'

'You're riling me up intentionally.'

'Maybe that's because I know what to do with you when you're angry. I felt powerless when you were so upset. I've never seen you like that before.'

And she'd be damned sure he never would again. Her chest heaved beneath the sensual silk. And some of her confusion billowed out.

'But that fire in your eyes and the sharpness of your words…? *That* I know.' He slid one arm around behind her and pulled her hard up against his chest. 'That and this feeling that I get when you're on fire.'

He took her hand and pressed it over his left pectoral muscle. His heart hammered wildly beneath it. 'Feel that? That's what you do to me. So please don't tell me I'm not attracted to you.'

She bent back as far as she could in his hold. Eyed him warily. Even as her own pulse began to gallop. 'You're just mad,' she muttered.

'Woman, you have no idea.'

He released her then and turned and crossed to the window. 'Audrey. You kill me. You have so much yet you don't value it. You don't see it.' He plunged both hands into his pockets as if to keep himself from reaching for her again. 'And I sit here every damned Christmas, wanting you, and wondering if you'd recognise the signs, if you had even the slightest clue that you were affecting me that way.'

Silence fell heavy and accusatory. But his outburst was enough to finally get the message through.

He was serious. He was actually drawn to her.

What the hell did she do with that?

'I'm sorry, Oliver.'

He turned back, all the anger gone now. 'I wasn't angling for an apology. I'm angry *for* you, not *at* you. That everything in life has led you to have such little faith in yourself despite all the amazing things you are. And I'm mad at myself that—despite everything my head tells me, despite the total lack of signals from you—my body just doesn't get the message.'

Her chest tightened like a fist.

No, he wasn't angry. He was hurting.

A lot.

'You never let on.'

'If there's one thing I'm good at, it's command over my baser instincts.'

She wet her lips and chewed them a little bit. This was Oliver: a man she cared for and respected. A man she'd been harbouring any number of inappropriate thoughts about for years. And he was telling her that the attraction was mutual.

'How could there be signals…?' she started.

He raised a hand to stop her. 'I understand, Audrey—'

'No, you don't. I meant how could I give you signals, when I was married and I knew how strongly you felt about fidelity? Above all else, I didn't want you to think badly of me.'

*Not you.*

He stared. 'Why would I?'

'You would have. If you could have seen into my head and read my thoughts sometimes when I was with you.'

Or lots of times when she wasn't.

He hadn't been moving before but somehow his body grew more still. Still and dangerously alert. 'What are you saying?'

'I'm saying that the absence of signals is a reflection of my great need for your good opinion.' She took a deep breath. 'Not my actual feelings.'

The shame in his gaze dissipated, heated and evaporated by the desire that took its place. But still he didn't move.

'You're not married now,' he murmured. 'And I'm hardly in a position to judge you given some of the fantasies I had when you were my friend's bride.'

Her breath tightened and ran out.

He was right. There was nothing stopping them. Blake was gone, and any loyalty she'd ever felt for him had dissolved the moment she discovered his serial infidelity. Oliver wasn't seeing anyone. She wasn't seeing anyone. They were both here in this amazing, private place. And she wouldn't see him again for twelve months.

And no one but them would know.

There was no reason in the world that she shouldn't cross

the empty space between them and put her hands on Oliver Harmer as she'd been dreaming of for years.

And that freedom was completely and utterly terrifying.

She crossed to the window, instead, stared out at the view. All those millions of people just going about their business, oblivious to the torment happening at the top of one of the hundreds of buildings lining their harbour.

'Did you just weird yourself out?' he murmured from behind her.

*Right* behind her.

He read her like a book. There wasn't a person alive who knew her as well as this man she only saw once a year. She smiled. 'Sure did.'

She could feel him there, his heat reaching out for her, but not touching. Just…teasing. Tormenting. Tantalising.

But she couldn't turn around to save her life. She clung to the ant-sized community far below them and used them as her anchor. Before she floated up and away on this bliss.

'It doesn't have to be weird,' he whispered. 'We're still the same people.'

That was exactly what made it weird. But also so very exciting. As her pounding pulse could attest.

'But you have to want it,' he breathed. 'And you have to think about it. I need you to make the conscious decision.'

'You want me to make the first move?' Please, no… surely?

'I want you to be certain.' His words brushed her ear.

She steadied herself with hands on the window, either side of her body, her hot palms instantly making a thermal handprint on the cool glass.

'What if I'm no good?' She hated how tiny her voice sounded.

The chuckle that rumbled in his chest so close behind her was almost close enough to feel. 'Audrey, I'm not even touching you and it's already good.'

He leaned more of his weight into her, pressing her to the window and the hard tension in his body gave his words veracity. The contrast of the cool glass to her front and his big, hot body at her back made her breath shudder in her throat.

'Let me show you.' His knuckle came up to stroke her hair back from her face, back over her shoulder. And it was that—more than anything he could have said or done— that convinced her.

Because those big, tan, confident fingers…?

They were trembling like an autumn leaf.

Her eyes fluttered shut and she forced all the doubts and fears and questions out of her mind and just let herself *feel*. The moment she tipped her head, exposing more of her throat above the delicate collar hem of the dress, Oliver dropped his lips straight onto her skin, hot and self-assured.

Her legs practically gave way. If not for the press of his body sandwiching her to the glass window she would have slid in a heap onto the expensive bamboo parquetry. Air shuddered in and out of her on inelegant gasps as his mouth and chin nuzzled below the blue and silver collar, then around to the front of her throat, lathing her collarbone. His hands covered hers on the glass and twisted them down to trace, with him, the silken length of her body.

His knuckles brushed the sides of her breasts, her waist, the swell of her hips, leaving her trembling and alive. Then he released her hands and one of his slipped around to press against her belly while the other traced down the outer curve of one buttock. Beneath its underside.

Her eyes flew open.

'Just feel it,' he murmured against her skin. 'Just be brave.'

The strange choice of words was lost again in the excruciating sensations of his lips back on her throat. They climbed up behind her ear, lingered there a moment and then drifted forward, across her jaw, along her cheek.

Searching. Seeking. And when they reached what they were seeking Audrey was more than ready for them.

His mouth pressed against hers on a masculine, throaty sigh, and she twisted slightly in his hold to improve her purchase and meet his exploration with her own.

Wave after wave of vertigo washed over her as she stood, pressed against nothing but open sky and man, all the air in her body escaping out to mingle with Oliver's. She clung to his lips as though they were the only thing stopping her from plunging sixty storeys.

He tasted exactly as she'd dreamed—decadent and masculine and delicious.

He felt just as she'd always imagined—hard and hot and in control.

But so, so much better. Like nothing she'd ever experienced in her life.

*Be brave*, he'd said. This was what he meant. Take a chance.

Embrace the risk.

She twisted fully in his grasp, pressing her back to the glass, and slid her arms up around his bent neck.

And she kissed him back for all she was worth.

Things really took off then. Oliver slid his foot between her feet and nudged them apart, making room for the expensive fabric of his thigh. That pressed against her everywhere she'd started to ache but it also took over the important job of holding her up, which freed his hands to roam the front of her body where they'd been unable to go moments before.

One plunged up into her hair and the other trailed its way up to a breast. And he relieved her of another ache, there, with a gentle squeeze.

He ripped his mouth from hers as fast as his hand snatched away from her breast. 'You're not wearing a bra?'

Confusion dazzled her, but she answered, 'It was in the

pile you sent for cleaning.' Some of the salsa had soaked through onto it. Which was a ridiculous thought to be having just now.

'That's going to make it a bit harder,' he gritted, blazing the words along the neglected side of her throat.

It was all she could do to harness enough air to keep speaking. 'Make what harder?'

'Stopping.'

'Why would you stop?'

Why *in this world*...?

'Because we're about to have company.'

She ripped her ear away from where his hot lips were torturing them. Company wasn't *just the two of them*. Company wasn't *no one will know*. Company was public. And she was standing with her skirt half hiked up sandwiched between Oliver and the window in the direct eyeline of the door.

He stepped back, but not without reluctance.

'What company?'

'I asked for the next dish to be served up here.'

'Why the hell would you do that?'

Well…wasn't she quite the lady when in the throes of carnal disappointment?

Moisture from her swollen lips glinted on his as he smiled. 'I didn't know this was going to happen. I thought you might have appreciated the privacy.'

She tugged her skirt down. He stepped back.

*Looks like stopping is all taken care of.* 'I would love privacy right now.'

'You don't have to eat it. We can resume the moment they're gone.' His gaze grew keen. 'If that's what you want.'

Was that what she wanted? Yes, right now it really was. Right now, she was numb all over except for some very dissatisfied, very grumpy, very pointed points of focus that couldn't really think of anything other than resuming. But in five minutes…who knew? By then her brain might have kicked back in and reminded her of all the reasons this was a bad, bad idea.

In five minutes this could all be over.

*You have to be certain.* That was what he'd said, and maybe this was what he'd meant. That she needed to be certain in the cold, hard light of reality, not the hot, fevered place he'd just taken her.

On cue, the door sounded slightly. She spun to face back out of the window, tugging her dress unnecessarily into position and pretending she'd just been admiring the view, not the sensation of Oliver's hand on the screaming flesh of her breast. Behind her, Oliver accepted the meal with thanks and closed the door quietly.

Then there was silence. So much silence that Audrey eventually turned around.

He stood, staring at her silhouette, the loaded tray balanced in his arms, a question on his face.

Giving her the choice.

Another bonus of being rich, he could ignore the just-delivered food, spend the evening trying out every soft surface in the place—and a few of the harder ones—and nothing would ever be said. At least not aloud.

If only the rest of the world worked that way.

Her pulse hadn't even had time to settle, yet. How could she make a good decision with it still screaming around her body with a swag of natural chemicals in tow?

She made her choice, curling one arm across her torso. 'What's under the lid?'

'Fingers of chilled ginger specially prepared.' If he was disappointed, he didn't let it show particularly. He quirked one eyebrow, deliciously, and wet the lips that had just done such gorgeous damage to hers. 'Want a taste, Audrey?'

Okay, so he wasn't going to let her go easily.

She smoothed her dress once again and then crossed

to the oversized dining table and slid into the seat at one corner. With no chair at the end he would either have to sit next to her or across from her. One was too close but she wouldn't have to look into those all-seeing eyes. The other...

Of course he chose that one, sinking into the seat immediately opposite.

'Stop thinking,' he murmured as he lifted the lid off the delivered tray and spread the contents between them on the table.

'I'm not.'

'You are. And you're partitioning. I can see it happening.' He served up the fanned palate cleanser. 'You're separating the parts of what just happened into acceptable and unacceptable and you're locking them in different boxes.'

She kept her eyes averted.

'But I'm curious to know what you put where.'

She lifted her gaze for an answer.

'Where did you file being here, with me, alone in this suite?'

She took a deep, slow breath. 'Being here is necessary. And sensible.' And therefore completely defensible.

'What about being in that dress?'

'The dress is beautiful. It makes me feel beautiful.' The door was wide open for him to say '*you are beautiful*'. But he didn't. Part of her was pleased that he didn't resort to trite niceties. A smaller part cried just a little bit.

He leaned back in the expensive chair and considered her. 'What would you change? If you could? If money was no object.'

She considered. The shape of her eyes wasn't anything to write home about unaided, but they came up pretty well under skilfully applied make-up. And their colour was harmless enough. Her lips were even and inoffensive, not too small, and they sat neatly under a long straight nose. Even that couldn't be called a problem, particularly.

It was just all so...lacklustre.

'My jaw's a bit square.'

He shook his head once. 'It's strong. Defined.'

'You asked me what I'd change. That's something.'

'It gives you character.'

She laughed. 'Yep. Because all women hunger to have a face "with character".'

'You can have character and still be beautiful. But okay, what else?'

She sighed. 'It's not a case of individual flaws. It's not like I could get a brow-lift or have my ears pinned and I'd feel reborn. It's just that I don't have...' She considered her wording options. 'There's no *standout* feature in my appearance.'

'I could name three.'

'Ha ha.'

'I'm serious. Want to hear them?'

She took a deep breath. Part of her wanted to watch him flounder, to make him own his lies. But a deeper part again wondered if he might see her differently from what she saw in the mirror. Curiosity won.

'Sure.'

'Your cheekbones,' he started, immediately, as though he'd been waiting years to say it. 'You don't highlight them, but you don't need to. And when you smile and your muscles contract their angle seems to intensify.'

She lifted one brow. 'Good to know.'

'And that's number two, despite the sarcasm. Your face is rich with...intelligence. You always look so switched on, so intent. That stands out for me, big time.'

'I have a smart face?'

'Anyone can have a garden-variety pretty face...'

She processed that. His body language said he was serious, but she wasn't about to make a fool of herself by getting all hot and bothered by his praise. 'Wow, I'm very curious to know what could possibly top a "smart" face...'

He didn't hesitate. 'Your body.'

Not what she was expecting. And the intent fixation of his gaze was just a little bit disconcerting. 'Please don't call me athletic.'

'No?' Which meant he'd been about to.

'That's code for "shapeless and flat-chested".'

'Only if you're looking for offence.' He considered her and his eyes darkened before he spoke. 'Here's what athletic means to me.'

He leaned slightly forward.

'Malleable. Flexible.' Every word was more of a breath. 'Resilient. Strong. It's a body that won't break easily under duress.'

The air flowing in and out of her lungs seemed to divest itself of oxygen and she had to increase her respiration to compensate. Her undisciplined imagination filled with images of the kind of duress he might be referring to. And ways of applying it.

'I think of endurance and fortitude—'

'Is everything about sex with you?' she breathed.

Pot. Kettle. Black.

'Who says I'm just talking about sex? What about a long, healthy life? What about childbirth? What about long hikes out there—' he indicated the steep slope of Hong Kong's wilderness trails on a distant green mountain '—and stretching out, long and straight on this sofa watching a movie? A man might see the surface details with his eyes, but his biology is naturally drawn to the kind of mate that will live as long as he does.'

The picture he painted was idyllic and she got the sense that that was exactly what he saw when he looked at her.

Potential.

Not flaws.

Awkwardness—and awareness—surged around them. She never was good with compliments, but there was also the sense that maybe he'd given the subject of her figure a whole lot more thought than just a few seconds.

'Although, yeah, it's definitely the kind of body that tends to make a man start thinking about getting sweaty.' Those thoughts reflected darkly in his eyes. 'And that's a whole other body part paying attention.'

Audrey grabbed the levity like a life raft on the sea of unspoken meaning on which she'd suddenly found herself adrift. 'That's what I figured.'

He joined her in that life raft. 'What can I say? I'm a man of very few dimensions.'

Not true. Not at all. And she was just beginning to get a sense of how much she'd yet to learn about him. And about how long that could take.

'I wish you could see yourself as I see you,' he murmured.

She shrugged. 'I don't lose sleep over it or anything.'

'I know. But I'd love to watch you walk into a room, full of knowing self-confidence instead of doubt.'

She knew exactly what he was talking about. Somewhere along the line she learned to downplay her strengths, maybe to fly under the radar. 'Confidence attracts you?'

'Completely.'

'Is that what the beautiful women are all about?'

'It's not their aesthetics I'm drawn to.'

No. She was starting to realise how shallow her accusation that *he* was shallow really was.

'But sadly the confidence doesn't always hold up. Some of them were the most fragile women I've ever met.'

'Maybe you just expect too much?' she risked.

'By knowing what I want?'

'By expecting it all. And maybe they got the sense that

they were failing to measure up to some undefined standard.'

He stared at her. 'Law of averages. If one woman can have everything I want, then there has to be another.'

She had *everything* he wanted? That was a whole lot more than just intellectual compatibility. Her heart thumped madly. 'And yet I lack the confidence you look for. So incomplete, after all.'

'I said you don't see it, not that you don't have it. You could own any room you walked into if you could just tap into your self-belief.'

If only it were *as easy* as turning on a tap. 'A few more conversations like this one and maybe I will.'

He looked inordinately pleased to have pleased her. 'I live to serve.'

The intensity of his gaze reached out and curled around her throat, cutting off most of her air. 'Really? Then how about serving me another finger?'

Oliver finished his dish way ahead of Audrey. She stalled, wiping up every drop, using it as a chance to cool things off as much as the ginger had. One part of her hungered for more of the physical sensation she'd enjoyed before the food came. Exactly as stimulating as the gastronomic marathon they were undertaking. But another part—the sensible, logical part—knew that there was much more going on with her than just Oliver's desire for some activity of the *athletic* kind.

And *more than* was a big mental shift to be making in one day. Particularly when she'd come here today all ready to say goodbye.

To cut off her supply.

'I think maybe we should head back downstairs,' she murmured.

That surprised him. 'Now?'

She folded her napkin neatly and placed it next to her licked-clean plate on the expensive table. 'I think so.'

'Safety in numbers, Audrey?'

'What happened before was—' *amazing, unprecedented, unforgettable* '—compelling, but I don't think we should necessarily pick up where we left off.'

It was too dangerous.

'You seemed as *compelled* as I was. Can you just walk away from it?'

'I… Yes. The timing is all wrong.'

'We're both single. We're alone in an executive suite looking out over one of the world's most beautiful views. We have the whole evening ahead of us. And it's Christmas. How could the timing be better?'

His knowing eyes saw way too much. Like just how much of a liar she was. 'I just learned my husband was cheating on me…' she hedged.

'I assumed you'd slipped into revenge sex mode.'

'You think me that much of a user?'

'Are you still a us*er* if the us*ee* is fully aware of what you're doing? I'd be delighted to be exploited for any revenge activity whatsoever.' He held his hands out to the side. 'Do your worst.'

Impossible man. And impossible to know if he was serious or joking, or some complicated combination of the two. 'That wouldn't be particularly mature, Oliver.'

'Sometimes the body knows better than the brain what it really wants. Or needs.'

'You think I *need* a good roll in the hay?' Did she strike him as that uptight?

'Who says I'm talking about you?'

*Oh, please.* 'Like you didn't have sex twice this week already.'

'I did not.'

'Then last week.'

He stared at her. Infuriatingly unabashed.

'Earlier in the month, then.'

'Nope.'

The mere concept of a celibate Oliver was fascinating. But she wasn't going to allow even intrigue. 'Well, that explains today's detour from the norm. You're horny.'

'Any detour we take today—' she didn't fail to notice his use of the future tense '—won't be due to lack of self-control on my part.'

'So bloody cocky,' she muttered, pulling the dishes together into an easy-to-collect pile for the hotel staff. 'And presumptuous if you think I lack self-discipline.'

It was another of the virtues she was prepared to own.

'Far from it. The moment I let you shore up your resolve, I'm screwed. You'll set your mind to leaving and I'll never see you again.'

A raw kind of tragedy lurked behind his eyes. 'So... you're keeping me off kilter, just to be safe?'

'Trying to.'

Huh. It was working. 'How is confessing that going to help your cause?'

'I'm trying something new. Something that goes against everything my instincts tell me.'

She narrowed her eyes at him.

'Honesty.'

'You're always honest with me.'

'I don't lie. That's not the same as being honest. There's a lot I don't say, rather than have to lie to you.'

'Like not telling me about Blake?'

'Like not telling you how badly I want you every time I see you.'

Air shot into her lungs in a short, sharp gasp.

'That's right, Audrey. Every single time. And it's not going to go away just because you refuse to think about it.'

Her chest pressed in on itself. 'I assume you don't want to go back downstairs?'

'I do not.' His gaze was resolute. 'We're too close.'

'Close to what?'

'Close to everything I've wanted for years.'

*Wanted.* Her, on a plate. It was still too inconceivable to trust. 'Regardless of what I want?'

'If I thought you didn't want it I'd be holding the door open for you right now and calling up the elevator.'

A fist squeezed around her larynx.

'But you do. You just need to let yourself have it.' He glowered down on her. 'And believe you deserve it.'

She curled her arms around the sensual silk of her loaned dress and remembered instantly how much better his arms had felt doing the same thing just minutes ago. *Deserve it?* Did he know what he was asking her to set aside? Years of careful, safe emotional shielding?

Of course she wanted to sleep with him. It seemed stupidly evident to her. But *dare* she? Could she do it and not be crippled by old doubts? Could she do it and not want more? Because he wasn't offering *more*. He was offering *now*.

And right now she had allure working very much in her favour.

'The Audrey of your imagination must be spectacular,' she whispered, enjoying the solar flare that erupted in his smouldering gaze. 'But, seriously, what if I'm just ordinary?'

Or worse. Was that something she could bear him knowing?

He stepped closer and slid his big hand around her cheek. 'Honey, I'm that keyed up I may not even notice what you're doing.'

A choked kind of laugh rattled through her. Bless Oliver

Harmer and his gift for putting her at ease. 'You're supposed to say, "You couldn't possibly be, Audrey".'

'You *couldn't* possibly be, Audrey,' he repeated, all seriousness. 'But I'm done enabling you. If you want to know for sure you're going to have to take a step. Take a risk.' He lowered his hand between them and stretched it towards her, his eyes blazing but steady. 'And take my hand.'

She stared at those long, talented, certain fingers. No trembling now.

If she slid her own in between them she was changing her life, going boldly where she'd never gone before.

A one-night stand.

Sex with Oliver.

That couldn't be undone. And it probably wouldn't be repeated; after all, they only saw each other once a year and a lot could change in twelve months.

*Revenge sex*, he'd joked. But was it so very funny? She certainly had enough to feel vengeful for. She'd wasted years being modest and appropriate and not throwing herself across the table at a scrumptious Oliver every year out of loyalty to a man who was betraying everything she'd ever stood for. Who couldn't wait for her to leave the country so he could express the man he really wanted to be.

Wasn't she due a little bit of payback?

And wouldn't that moment when Oliver strained over her just as he had in her most secret fantasies…wouldn't *that moment* undo everything that had gone before it? Wouldn't she be reborn?

Like a phoenix out of the ashes of her ridiculous, restrained life.

His fingers twitched, just slightly, out there all alone in the gulf of inches between them and the simple movement softened her heart.

This wasn't sleazy. This wasn't some kind of set-up or

test and there wasn't a bunch of schoolgirls waiting to slam her up against the bathroom wall for daring to reach.

This was Oliver.

And *he* was reaching for *her.*

She lifted her eyes, fastened them to his cautious hazel depths and slid her fingers carefully between his.

# CHAPTER TEN

*Lavender-cured crocodile, watermelon fennel salad
served with a lime emulsion*

'AGAIN?'

Audrey's beautiful, sweat-slicked chest rose and fell
right in Oliver's peripheral vision as she sprawled, wild
and indelicate, across his bed, eyeing him lasciviously.

His laugh strangled deep in his throat. 'I won't be doing
it again for a little bit, love.'

'Really? You're not a three-times-a-night kind of guy?'

He rolled over and stared at her. 'Have you never heard
of recovery? Any man who can go three times in a row
didn't do it thoroughly the first time.'

And she'd been done *extremely* thoroughly.

The second time, anyway.

Their first time had been hot, and hard and slick and
they didn't even make it off the sumptuous sofa. He'd been
joking about being so keyed up, but it had taken a gargan-
tuan effort on his part to keep things at a pace that wouldn't
scare her off forever.

Or shame him.

The second time they'd turned nomad; roaming from
surface to surface, view to view, stretching out the torture,
exploring and learning the geography of each other's bodies,
knocking vases off tables and sending light fittings swing-

ing. He'd been determined to make a slightly better—and lengthier—showing than the almost adolescent fumblings on the sofa, and Audrey had risen to the challenge like the goddess she was, matching him move for move, touch for touch.

Until they'd finally collapsed in a heap on the penthouse's luxurious master bed where he really got to show her how he'd earned his nickname.

He rolled his exhausted head towards her. 'You were kidding, right?'

'Hell, yes. I'm numb.'

*There we go...* That was what a man liked to hear. He flipped his arm with the last remnants of energy he had and patted her unceremoniously on her perfect, naked bottom.

'Take that, Blake,' she said, after the giggles had subsided.

Audrey giggling. Wasn't that one of the heralds of the apocalypse?

'Hell hath no fury...' But it wasn't about vengeance, he knew that. This was much more fundamental.

'It wasn't me,' she whispered to the ceiling. And to every demon still haunting her.

He gave her a gentle shove with his own damp shoulder. 'Told you.'

'Yeah, you did.'

'Do you believe me now?'

'Yeah.' She sighed. 'I do.'

Then more silence.

Oliver studied the intricate plasterwork above them and mulled over words he'd never needed—or wanted—to utter. Found himself inexplicably nervous and utterly shamed of his own cowardice.

*So...now what happens?*

That was what he wanted to know. Half dreading and half breathless with anticipation at the answer. Because this—what they'd just shared—would be a crime to walk away from. He'd just had his deepest desire handed to him on a plate. Writhing under him.

Yet, he didn't do long-term. He didn't dare. Would he even know how? He'd lost years waiting for a woman with the right combination of qualities to come along. Goodness and curiosity and brilliance and elegance and wild, unbridled sensuality all bundled into one goddess.

He just wasn't going to find a woman on the planet better suited to being his.

Which meant he could *have* this remarkable gift that the universe had provided, but he couldn't *keep* it.

Because Audrey was far too precious to risk on someone as damaged as him.

Sex changed people. Women especially. Women like Audrey doubly especially. She wasn't a virgin, but he'd put good money on tonight being the first good sexual experience she'd had—again that sad, needy little troll deep inside him waved its club-fists triumphantly—and transformative experiences tended to make women start thinking of the future. Planning.

And he didn't do futures. He just couldn't.

There was more than one way of cheating in a relationship. He might never have been actually unfaithful to any of the women he'd been involved with, but he'd been false with every single one of them by not telling them they weren't measuring up to the bar set by a woman they'd never meet. By not telling them that what was between them was only ever going to be superficial.

By not telling them he wasn't in it for keeps.

He could dress it up whatever way he wanted—persevering, giving them a chance, getting to know one another—but the reality was from the moment he first realised they weren't the one, the rest of their time together was one big cheat.

As unfaithful and as unkind as his father. To every single one of them.

And so he'd come to specialise in short-term. He reserved his longest relationships for women who didn't change from first date to last. Predictable women who weren't looking for more. They got entire months.

Audrey wasn't the sort of woman you just kissed and farewelled after a few hot weeks. Look at the lengths he'd already gone to not to farewell her *at all*.

Audrey was someone he cared about deeply. And what happened from here was going to be critical to her remaining someone he was allowed to care deeply about. Because not caring for her was simply not an option. He couldn't even imagine it.

But using her—hurting her—wasn't going to work, either. He'd grown up witness to what it did to a woman to be in a relationship with a man incapable of loving just her.

It rotted her slowly from the inside out.

Bad enough imagining Audrey decaying in her sham of a marriage, but to think of himself being responsible for it… Watching her eyes getting dimmer and dimmer as he emotionally checked out of their relationship.

As he always did.

No. That was not something he was prepared to do to a woman he considered perfection. Who he actually cared for. Who he might love if he had any idea what the hell that meant.

And given his genetic make-up, the chances of him finding out any time soon weren't high.

But lying here drowning in *what-ifs* wasn't going to get them anywhere. Better to get it out in the open. Talk it through. Deal with whatever angst came.

*Just ask!*

'So what happens now?' he ground out. The longest four words of his life.

'Depends on what time it is.'

Okay. Uh, *not* what he was expecting. He craned his neck to check his TAG. 'Coming up to six p.m.'

Which meant she'd been here for eight hours already.

She rolled over, folding her arms under her as she went and boosting her breasts up into tantalising pillows. 'We still have half a degustation to enjoy.'

The little troll's fists fell limply by his side. She was thinking about food? While he was lying here doing a great impersonation of an angsty fourteen-year-old? 'Really? This hasn't been an adequate substitute?'

Her Mona Lisa smile gave nothing away. 'You said yourself we need to recharge. Might as well stretch our legs and eat while we do that.'

Stretch their legs. As if they'd just had a busy afternoon at their desks. He studied her for signs of weirdness—more than the usual amount—but found none. Her eyes were clear and untroubled.

'You're actually hungry?' Oh, my God, she actually was. Audrey Devaney might just be the perfect woman.

'Ravenous,' she purred. "That was quite a workout.'

No wonder he adored her. 'You want to be served up here?'

A hint of shadow crossed her expression. 'No. Let's go back downstairs.' But then she sagged and her warm lips fell against the cooling sweat of his shoulder. 'In just a minute or two.'


She was pretty hungry but, more than anything, Audrey wanted to walk back into this public restaurant with Oliver.

*With* Oliver.

Just for the sheer pleasure of doing it. Nothing but her dress had changed for the restaurant patrons or the staff because most of them probably assumed she and Oliver were already sleeping together. But *she'd* changed. *She* would know what it was like to have the best sex of her life with a man like Oliver Harmer, right over their very heads, and then casually stroll back in for the next course.

It was more decadent a sensation than if they'd served her palate cleanser smeared on Oliver's naked torso.

She stumbled over that image slightly and the fingers curled around hers tightened.

'Okay?'

She threw her gratitude sideways on a breathy acknowledgement. Lord, when had she become so…Marilyn Monroe?

She glanced awkwardly to the other tables for a half-heartbeat. Did she look like a woman who was quite accustomed to having exquisite sex between courses? *Could* she look like that? And it was, hands down, the best sex she'd ever had. With her husband. With anyone else. Even on her own. Her body was still swollen and sensitive and really, really pleased with itself.

What if she looked as smug as she felt?

'Are you sure you're okay?'

'I don't know what the etiquette is,' she admitted, dragging her focus back to their private little corner by the dragonflies as they approached. Were the insects this vivid and lively before or was everything just super-sensory right now?

'To what?'

'To walking into a room after our…bonus course.'

His chuckle eased a little of her nerves. 'I don't think there are any rules for that. You're going to have to wing it.'

'I feel—' *transformed* '—conspicuous.'

'If people are looking at you it's because of the dress, Audrey.'

Right. Not some tattoo on her forehead that said, 'Guess where she's just had her mouth.'

She sank, on instinct, towards her comfortable sofa and Oliver tugged on their still-entwined fingers as he kept moving.

Oh. *Together.*

How odd that—despite everything they'd done with each other and been to each other over the past hours—it was *this* that felt taboo. Like crossing over to the dark side. She joined Oliver on his sofa, facing the other way for the first time in five years, while he scanned her for the first sign of trouble.

She must look as if she was ready to bolt from the room.

She stretched, cat-like, back into his sofa. 'This is quite comfortable, too.'

'I've always liked it.'

Her bottom wriggle dug her a little deeper. 'I think you had the better end of the deal, actually.'

'I would definitely say so, today.'

Sweet.

Terrifying…but sweet.

Oliver did little more than flick his chin at a passing server and the man reappeared a moment later with two glasses of chilled white wine. Audrey smiled her thanks before sweeping her glass up and turning her attention again to the busy dragonflies in the tank that usually sat behind her, and, through its glass sides, the bustling kitchen on the far side of the restaurant.

'I always thought you were terribly sophisticated, knowing the timing of everything in a Michelin-starred restaurant,' she murmured. 'But you were cheating. You can see them coming.'

'It seems it's a night for exposing secrets.'

That brought her eyes back to his. 'Yes indeed.'

'Do you want to talk about it?'

*It.*

'I don't want to ruin it.' Or jinx it. 'But I don't want you to think I'm avoiding conversation, either.'

'Would you like to talk about something else?'

Desperately. 'What?'

He cupped his wine and leaned back into the corner of the sofa more comfortably. 'Tell me about the Testore.'

The instruments she hunted were certainly something she could get excited about. And talk about until his ears bled. 'What would you like to know?'

'How was it stolen?'

'Directly from the cabin of a commercial airline between Helsinki and Madrid, while the owner used the washrooms.'

'In front of a plane full of people?'

'The cabin was darkened. But Testores get their own seat when they fly so it's unusual that no one saw it being removed. Someone would have had to lean right over into the window seat.'

'Wow, it's that valuable? How did they get it off the plane without being seen?'

'No one knows. We have to assume one of the ground crew was paid off. The plane's cabin security picked up a shadow lingering by the seats and taking it but it was too dark to identify even gender. And short of paying for a seat for the instrument *and* one for a bodyguard I'm not sure what the owner could have done differently. She had to pee. They searched the plane top to bottom.'

The public areas, anyway.

'So how did you begin tracking it down?'

This was what she did. This was what she loved. It wasn't hard to relax and bore Oliver senseless with the details of her hunt for the cello.

Except that he didn't bore easily, clearly. Forty minutes later he was still engaged and asking questions. She'd kicked off her shoes again and tucked her feet up under her, feeling very much the Chinese waif in her silken sheath, helping herself to finger-sized portions of the crocodile and watermelon that was course number seven.

'Can you talk about all of this? Legally?' Oliver queried.

'I haven't told you anything confidential. It's all process.' She smiled. 'Plus I think I can trust you.'

His eyes refocused sharply, as if he had something to say about that, but then he released her from his fixed gaze and reached, instead, to trace the line of her arm with a knuckle. 'Your patience amazes me. And that you're so close to finding it when you started with practically nothing.'

Oh, he had no idea how patient she could be. Just look how long she'd endured her feelings for him. Or how long she could endure his tantalising touch before shattering.

Apparently.

'It's taken all year but we're just one step behind them now. The plan is to get ahead and then we have them. The authorities just have to wait for them to deliver it up.'

'Why don't these people just take it and go to ground for a decade? Put it in a basement somewhere? Hoard it?'

'Criminals aren't that patient for their money and, besides, their industry is full of loose lips. You steal something like a Testore and don't keep it moving and one of your colleagues is just as likely to steal it out from under you.'

'I really don't see the point.'

'Neither do I,' she admitted. 'Why have lovely things if you never see them?'

'I'm surprised the bad guys haven't tried to buy you off.'

'Oh, they've tried.' She smiled. 'My sense of natural justice is just too strong. And I view the instruments a bit like children. Innocent victims. Stolen. Abused. All they want to do is go home to the person that loves and values them and keeps them safe and fulfils their potential.'

Because wasn't that what life was all about? Fulfilling your potential.

The brown in his eyes suddenly seemed more prominent. And chocolaty. And much closer. Which one of them had moved so subtly? Or had they both just gravitated naturally together?

'Want to hear something dumb?' he murmured.

'Sure.'

'That's how I feel about the companies I buy.'

She flicked an eyebrow. 'The near-crippled companies you get for a song, you mean?'

He smiled. 'They're innocent victims, too. In the hands of people that don't value them and don't understand how to make them strong.'

'And you do?'

'I'm like you—a facilitator. I have the expertise to recognise the signs of a flailing business and I gather them up, strengthen them and get them to the people who can give them a future.'

'That's a very anthropomorphic belief.'

'Says the woman who thinks of a cello like a trafficked child.'

She smiled. He was right. 'You don't ever break them up?'

'Not unless they're already falling to pieces.'

That was her greatest fear. Finding an instrument that someone took to with a sledgehammer rather than relinquish. Because some people were just like that: if they couldn't have it, no one would.

'I'm guessing that the people you buy them from don't see it that way.'

He shrugged. 'Hey, they're the ones selling. No one's forcing them.'

'I guess I hadn't realised how similar our jobs are.

Though I get the feeling yours has a lot more facets.' Like a diamond. It was certainly worth a whole heap more.

Oliver studied her as he finished the last of the watermelon. 'That wasn't so bad, was it?'

'What?'

'Having a conversation.'

'We've had lots of conversations.'

'Yet somehow that feels like our first.'

It did have that exciting hum about it. 'I miss conversation.'

'Blake's been gone a while.'

'I never really talked with him. Not like this.' Not like Oliver. 'So it's been a couple of years.'

'Did you move to Antarctica when I wasn't looking? What about your friends?'

'Of course I have friends. And we talk a lot, but they've all known me forever and so our conversation tends to be about…you know…stuff. Mutual friends. Work. Dramas. Clothes.'

'That's it?'

'That's a lot!' But those steady hazel eyes filled her with confidence. 'I'm not… I don't share much. Often.' And she could never talk about Oliver. To anyone.

'You share with me.'

'Once a year. Like cramming.' Did that even count?

Nothing changed in his expression yet everything did. He studied her, sideways, and then reached out to drag soft knuckles across the back of her hand. 'You call me up whenever you want. I'd love to talk to you more often. Or email.'

The cold, hard wash of reality welled up around her.

Right. Because she was leaving in the morning. As she always did. Flying seven thousand kilometres in one direction while he flew twelve hundred in the other. Back to their respective lives.

Back to reality. With a phone plan.

'Maybe I will.'

Or maybe she'd chalk tonight up to a fantastic one-night stand and run a million miles from these feelings. That could work.

A murmuring behind them drew Oliver's gaze.

'Hey, it's starting.'

No need to ask what 'it' was. Her favourite part of December twentieth. Her favourite part of Christmas. Oliver pulled her to her feet and she padded, barefoot, on the luxury carpet to the enormous window facing Victoria Harbour. Below them Hong Kong's nightly light show prepared to commence.

Both sides of the harbour lit up like a Christmas tree and pulsed with the commencement of music that the Qīngtíng suddenly piped through their sound system. Massive lighting arrays, specially installed on every building the length of both sides of the waterfront, began to strobe and dance. It wasn't intended to be a Christmas show but, to Audrey, it couldn't be more so if it were set to carols. She couldn't see a light show anywhere without thinking about this city.

This man.

Oliver slipped her in front of him between the window and the warmth of his body and looped his arms across her front, and she knew this was the light show she'd be remembering on her deathbed.

Emotion choked her breathing as she struggled to keep the rise and fall of her chest carefully regulated. Giving nothing away. The beautiful lights, the beautiful night, the beautiful man. All wrapped around her in a sensory overload. Wasn't this what she'd wanted her whole life? Even during her marriage?

Belonging.

Never mind that it was only temporary belonging; she'd take what she could get.

'I missed this so much last year,' she breathed.

His low words rumbled against her back. 'I missed you.'

The press of her cheek into his arm was a silent apology. 'Let's just focus on tonight.'

She wasn't going to waste their precious time dwelling on the past or dreaming of endless combinations of futures. She had Oliver right here, right now; something she never could have imagined.

And she was taking it. While she could.

'What time does Qīngtíng close?'

His body tensed behind her. 'Got a flight to catch?'

She turned her head, just slightly—away from the light show, away from the other patrons, back towards him. 'I want to be alone with you.'

'We can go back upstairs.'

She took a breath. Took a chance. 'No, I want to be alone, here.'

Okay, that was definitely tension radiating on the slow hiss he released as a curse.

Too much? Had she crossed some kind of he-man line? She turned back to the view as though that was all they'd been discussing. As though it were that meaningless. But every cell in her body geared for rejection and made her smile tight. 'Or not.'

Oliver curled forward, lips hard against her ear. 'Don't move.'

And then he was gone, leaving her with only her own, puny arms to curl around her torso.

Ugh. She was so ill equipped for seduction.

And for taking a risk.

It was only moments before he returned, assuming his previous position and tightening his hold as though he'd never been gone. So… Maybe okay, then? It wasn't a total retreat on his part. The show went on, spectacular and epic, but all Audrey could think about was the press of Oliver's hips against her bottom. His hard chest against her back and how that had felt pressing onto her front not too long ago.

Light show? What light show?

At last, she recognised the part of the music that heralded the end of the nightly extravaganza and she tuned in once again to the sounds around her, reluctant to abandon the warm envelope of sensory oblivion she'd shared with Oliver in the dark.

Like insects scuttling away from sudden exposure, a swarm of staff whipped the restaurant's dishes and themselves back behind closed doors as the lights gently rose. The maître d' spoke quietly in turn to the six remaining couples and each of them collected up their things, curious acceptance on their faces, and within moments were gone.

'Oliver—?'

'Apparently your wish is my command.'

Her mouth gaped in a very unladylike fashion. 'Did you throw them out?'

'A sudden and unfortunate failure in the kitchen and a full return voucher for each of them. I'm sure they're thrilled.'

'Considering they were nearly on their last course—' and considering what Qīngtíng's degustation cost '—I'm sure they are, too.'

He led her back to his sofa.

Ming-húa appeared with a full bottle of white wine, an elegant pitcher of iced water and a remote control and placed all three on the table before murmuring, 'Goodnight, Mr Harmer. Mrs Audrey.'

And then he was gone back through the kitchen and out whatever back-of-house door the rest of the staff had discreetly exited through.

She turned her amazement to him in the luminous glow of the dragonfly habitat.

'Just like that?'

'They'll get it all cleaned up before the breakfast opening.'

Uh-huh. Just like that. 'Do you always get what you want?'

'Mostly. I thought you wanted it, too.'

'Wanting and getting aren't usually quite that intrinsically linked in my world.'

'Have you changed your mind?'

'Well…not exactly…' Although her breathless words were easier to own in the dark with the press of his body for motivation.

He leaned back into the luxury sofa and threw her a knowing look. 'You're all talk, Devaney.'

'I am not. I'm just thrown by the expedience with which that was…dealt with.'

'Careful what you wish for, then, because you might get it.'

Alone again.

Audrey glanced around the stylish venue. Then at the door. Then at Oliver.

His eyes narrowed. 'What?'

'I just need a minute…'

She pushed again to her bare feet and strolled casually to the far side of the restaurant, and considered it before turning.

'Lost something?'

'I'm just seeing how the other half live.'

She peered out of the glass. Their view was definitely better in the dragonfly corner. Although it was, of course, exactly the same. Except Oliver was part of her view over there.

He chuckled and settled back to watch her. She hiked the sensuous fabric of her loaned dress up her legs slightly and then *cantered*—there was no other word for it—around the restaurant usually bustling with people.

'You're mad,' he chuckled, struggling to keep his eyes off her bared legs.

'No, I'm snoopy.'

She stuck her head inside the servery window and checked out the glamorous kitchen. No food left out overnight but definitely a clean-up job for someone in the morning. An industrial dishwasher did its thing somewhere in the corner, humming and churning in the silence.

On a final pass by his sofa, Oliver stretched up and snagged her around the waist, dragging her, like the prey of a funnel-web spider, down into the lair of his lap. Her squeal of protest was soaked up by the luxurious carpet and furnishings.

'Do they have security cameras?'

'Do you imagine they're not fully aware of why I sent them home early?'

The idea that they were all stepping out into the street, glancing back up at the top of their building and imagining—

Heat rushed up where Oliver's lazy strokes were already causing a riot. 'There's a big difference between knowing and seeing. Or sharing on YouTube.'

'Relax. Security is only on the access points, fire escape and the safe. The only audience we have are of the invertebrate variety.'

Her eyes went straight to the pretty dragonflies now extra busy in their tank, as though they knew full well when the staff left for the evening and were only just now emerging for their nightly party.

Oliver reached with the hand not doing such a sterling job of feeling her up and pressed the small, dark remote control. The restaurant lights immediately dimmed to the preset from the light show.

'There you go. We'll be as anonymous as your Testore thief on their flight.'

Lying here in the dark, lit only by the dragonflies and the lights of Hong Kong outside, it was easy to imagine they were invisible.

'So—' he settled her more firmly against his body and made sure that they were connecting in dozens of hot, hard places '—you were saying? About being alone?'

'We have such a short time,' she whispered. 'I didn't want to share you with a crowd.'

A shadow ghosted across his eyes before they darkened, warmed and dropped towards her. 'The feeling is entirely mutual.'

His lips on hers were as soft, as pliable as before, but warmer somehow and gentler. As if they had all the time in the world instead of just a few short hours. She kissed him back, savouring the taste and feel of him and taking the time neither of them had taken upstairs. He didn't escalate, apparently as content to enjoy the moment as she was.

She hadn't indulged in a good old-fashioned make-out session since her teens. And even that hadn't been all that good, truth be told.

But neither of them were superheroes. Before long, her breath grew as tight as the skin of her body and a suffusing kind of heat swilled around and between them. Oliver shed his dinner coat and Audrey scrunched the long, silk dress higher up her thighs in a sad attempt at some ventilation where it counted.

'I feel like a kid,' he rasped, 'making out in the back of his parents' car.'

'Except you know you'll be scoring at the end of the night.' And he already had, twice.

He smiled against her skin. 'With you I'm not taking anything for granted.'

She levered herself up for a heartbeat, let some much-needed air flush in between their bodies and then resettled against him. 'Come on. We both know I'm a sure bet.'

His head-back laugh only opened up a whole new bit of flesh for her to explore and so she did, dragging aching lips down his jaw and across his throat and Adam's apple. He tasted of salt and cologne. The best dish yet.

They lay like that—wrapped up in each other, all hands and lips, getting hot and heavy—for the better part of an hour. Long enough for the ice in the wine bucket to mostly melt away and Audrey to drink the entire contents of the still water Ming-húa had delivered.

'I hope you're not going to get too drunk to be any good to me,' she teased, when Oliver reached for the wine bottle. But he just winked, placing it on the table, and then dunked his glass straight into the fresh, melted ice in the bucket.

'Someone's drunk all the water,' he pointed out. 'And you have to stay hydrated in a marathon.'

'Is that what we're doing? An endurance event?'

'Well, I sure am.' He tossed the water back in one long swallow and a rivulet escaped and ran down his jaw. When his mouth returned to hers it was fresh and straight-from-the-ice-bucket cool.

It didn't last ten seconds.

They kissed a while longer but, even with her eyes closed and her mind very much otherwise occupied, she could feel the subtle shift of Oliver's body as he leaned towards the table. A moment later, he pulled his mouth from hers and placed a half-melted ice block on her swollen lips.

Her whole body lurched as he ran the icy surprise over her top lip and then her lower one, and she lapped at the trickle of melted water that ran into her mouth, smiling as he departed for her chin. Then her throat. Then around to the thumping pulse-point at the top of her jaw. His lips trailed a heartbeat behind the melting cube, kissing off the moisture as the ice liquefied against her scorching skin until it was completely gone.

Four cool fingers slid up her thigh and tucked under the

hem of her underwear while his other hand made a complete mess of her hair.

'Those girls at school must have known what they were doing,' he murmured hard against the ear he was lavishing.

'What do you mean?' She could barely remember them, and that was saying something.

'Even as kids, they must have known a threat when they saw one. That you were capable of this.'

His fingers moved further into her underwear. Into her. She arched into his touch. 'Such shamelessness?'

Greenish-brown eyes blazed into hers. 'Such potential passion. And, yeah, a hint of shamelessness. No wonder the boys finally caught on.'

She couldn't tell him she was packing a lifetime into this one night of the year. That she was hanging *way* outside her comfort zone because she knew she'd be spending the rest of her life safely inside it. Because how was she ever going to find something like this again, now that she'd tasted it?

Outside this day—outside this building—the real world ruled. It was a place where the kind of secret emotions she'd always harboured for sexy Oliver Harmer had no place being aired. And definitely not being indulged.

This was a 'what happens at Christmas stays at Christmas' kind of arrangement.

Casual and easy and terribly grown-up.

And the clock was ticking.

She moved against him to give him better access.

She'd grown lazy harbouring the feelings deep inside, exploiting the fact that he was *safe* to have feelings about as long as she was married. Like some kind of Hollywood star that it was okay to pant after because you knew you'd never, ever be acting on it. She held them close to her chest—clutched desperately, really—and enjoyed the sensations they brought. Enjoyed the what-if. Enjoyed the secret fantasy.

*Careful what you wish for,* he'd said.

But while she didn't dare indulge the emotional part, she was free to feed the physical part. The safe part. And Oliver was clearly very much up for the same with the hours they had left.

Because what happened here, inside the walls of this building, had nothing to do with the real world. And maybe it never had. Perhaps it had always been their weird little Cone-of-alternate-reality-Silence.

Maybe that was what made it so great.

'The synapses in your brain are smouldering,' he breathed, sniffing in amongst her hair. 'Stop overthinking this.'

'I can't help it,' she gasped. 'I'm a thinker.'

'Everyday-Audrey is a thinker. Go back to during-the-light show-Audrey. She was an impulsive and impressive doer.'

There you go. He saw it, too. There was a different set of rules for this day compared to the three hundred and sixty-four around it.

She twisted in his hold and it only pulled her dress up higher. But since both of them would have much preferred her to be out of it, that wasn't really a problem.

'You're right,' she said, settling more fully against him. 'Enough of the thinking. Let's go back to the feeling.'

Oliver pulled her more fully on top of him and studied her flushed face and shambolic hair.

'Best view ever,' he murmured.

'That's a big call given what's outside the window.'

He craned his neck towards the view. 'Good point. Change of plans.' His warm hand slid into hers. 'And change of view.'

She struggled to her feet alongside him, and Oliver led her, hand in hand, to an expensive, stuffed smoking chair by the window. One she'd always imagined him sitting in while he waited for her to arrive.

He twisted it square on to the view and sat before reaching for her.

'Where were we?'

'Here?' From first-sex to chair-sex in just a few hours. Alice was well and truly down the rabbit hole tonight.

'I wanted this upstairs. I've wanted it for years. You against that view. This is close enough.'

Her skin immediately remembered the cold press of glass against her hot breasts as he'd leaned on her from behind, upstairs, and her nipples hardened. There might not be the same drop sensation here on the chair a few feet back from all that glass and sky, but her stomach was doing enough flip-flops to qualify.

He took her hand and pulled her towards his lap. As she had on the sofa, she shimmied her silk dress higher to get her knees either side of his and then braced herself there.

'God, you're beautiful,' he breathed. 'Lit by all the lights of Hong Kong. It's like a halo.'

Was there a smoother-talking man in all this world? But her body totally fell for it, parts of her softening and throbbing an echo to the honey in his voice and the promise in his eyes. She lowered herself onto his lap.

One masculine hand slid, fully spread, up the tight, silk fabric of her stomach and over her breasts while the other followed it on the other side of her body, trailing the line of the dress's zip like someone following a rail line to the nearest town. At its end point he snagged the slider and lowered it and her loaner dress immediately loosened. It was a matter of moments before the hand at her breasts curled in the sensuous fabric and gently pulled it down her arms, revealing her uncovered breasts, and letting the beautiful fabric that he'd heated with his mere touch bunch, forgotten, around her waist.

'Oliver...' she breathed.

Two hands slid up her naked back holding her close as his body closed the gap between theirs and his mouth moved immediately to her breast, dined there, sucking and coiling and working his magic against the sensitive pucker of nipple.

Her skin bloomed with gooseflesh.

She twisted against the excruciating pleasure and indulged herself by doing something she'd always dreamed of—burying her fingers deep in his dark hair. Over and over, curling and tangling and tugging; luxuriating as he tortured the breasts that had barely seen sun with the rasping caress of stubble.

Her legs officially gave out, but the warmth of his lap was waiting to catch her.

As soon as she pressed down into him, his mouth came away, sought hers out and clung there, rediscovering her before dropping again to the other breast.

Behind him, the polished glass of the dragonfly habitat reflected them both against the beauty of the city skyline. She, a half-naked silhouette balanced wantonly on Oliver's lap, and he, pressed powerfully to her chest, with the stunning beauty of the Hong Kong skyline stretching out behind them. She looked wild and provocative and utterly alien to herself.

*This is what Oliver sees.*

This was how he saw her.

Liberation rushed through her. She didn't look ridiculous. She didn't look all wrong teetering on the expensive chair. Or not enough like the beautiful people he mixed with. She looked *just like* a beautiful person. She looked absolutely, one hundred per cent right bedded within Oliver's embrace.

They fitted together.

Deep in her soul, something cracked and broke away on

a tidal surge of emotion. Part of a levee wall, a giant fragment of whatever powerful thing had been holding back all her feelings all this time.

They *belonged* together.

And finally they were.

Oliver's silhouette hands released her at the back and reached up to pull the struggling pins from her hair, sending it tumbling down over her bare shoulders, tickling the tops of her bared breasts. His hands framed her face and drew her gaze back down to his, hot and blazing and totally focused.

Those eyes that promised her the world. Promised her forever.

And he was the only man she could imagine delivering it.

His lips, when she met them, were as hot and urgent as the touch that skittered over her flesh, and while she was distracted with that he levered them both up long enough to get his wallet out of his trousers pocket, fumbled in it for a moment then threw the whole thing on the floor.

'How many of those do you have?' she breathed, needing the moment of sanity to ground her spinning mind. Nothing like a condom to bring things screaming back to reality.

'Just the one.'

Disappointment warred with pleasure. *One* was a very finite number. The two he'd used upstairs came from a stash in the en suite cabinet, which might as well be back in Shanghai for all the use it was to them at this moment. Upstairs was a whole world away. But *one* also meant he didn't carry a string of *twelve* in case he found himself on a desert island with a life raft full of flight attendants.

Which was strangely reassuring.

As though *one* made tonight somehow less casual, for him.

But clarity streamed in with the fresh air. That was crazy

thinking. The fact he had a condom at all made it casual. The fact she was leaving for another country in a few hours made it casual. The fact Oliver didn't do relationships made it casual.

But whatever it was. She still wanted it. Come what may.

And she was taking it.

She lowered herself to mere millimetres from his lips and breathed against them. 'Don't break it.'

His chuckle was lost in the resumption of their hot kiss and her brain had to let go of such trivialities as what happened with the condom as it focused on the rush of sensation birthed by his talented fingers and lips. The strength with which he pulled her against his hard body. The expediency with which he solved the barriers of fabric between them. She pressed back up onto her knees to give him room to manoeuvre beneath her and then he shifted lower in the chair just slightly—just enough—and used one hand at her coccyx to steady her while another worked at the wet juncture of her thighs to guide her down onto the rigid, strength of him.

'So damned beautiful...'

His choked words only made her hotter. As it had been the first time, and the second, it was again now—like pulling on a custom-made kid glove. They fitted together perfectly. More perfectly than before, if that was possible, because gravity gave her extra fit. She rose up on her knees again, repositioned, and then sank fully down onto him, heavy and certain.

His throaty, appreciative groan rumbled through them both. Had there ever been a more heartening sound? How was it possible to feel so small and feminine and so strong and powerful at the same time? Yet she did, balanced on him like a jockey on a thoroughbred, with just as much control of the powerful beast below her through the subtle movements of her body.

She tipped her pelvis on a series of rocks and let the choked noises coming from his throat set the tempo. Steady, heavy, slow.

His head pressed back against the armchair as she ground against him, and Audrey curled forwards to trail her mouth across the exposed strength of his throat, exploring the hollow below it. Her position meant her breasts hung within easy reach of his taskless hands so he pressed them both against her flesh—as though they were the fulsome mounds he'd always secretly coveted, as though they were all his big hands could manage—circling his palms in big, hard arcs that mirrored the rhythm of her hips.

The desperate roughness of her want.

'Oliver…'

As her speed increased so did their breathing, and she arched back in his hold. In the terrarium glass, dragonflies buzzed around her reflection like fluorescent faeries…or like living sparks generated by the extraordinary friction of their bodies. Oliver's hands tightened and rubbed her straining breasts and every quivering massage told her how much closer to the edge he was getting. His excitement fuelled hers.

She was doing this to him.

*Her.*

As she watched the lithe undulations of their silhouette, tight heat coiled into an exquisite pain where they fused together and the armchair rocked with the combined momentum of their frantic bodies.

Up…

Up…

She tipped her head back and vocalised—an expressive, inarticulate, erotic kind of gurgle—as the fibres of her muscles bunched and readied themselves deep inside.

'Now, beautiful,' he strained on a grimace, meeting her

with the powerful upwards slam of his own hips. 'Come for me now.'

Her eyes snapped down to his—unguarded and raw— she let her soul pour out of them.

And then her world imploded.

As if the top storeys of their hotel had just *sheared away* in a landslide, and she went careening down to the earth far below on a roller-coaster tide of molten, magnificent mud. Punishing and protective. Weakening and reinforcing. Twitching and spasming. Utterly overwhelming.

She opened her eyes just in time to see them reflected in the tank, as glittering and ancient as the creatures flying around in it, and just in time to see the torsion of Oliver's big body beneath hers as he came right after her.

A pained stream of air, frozen on the prolonged first consonant of an oath and lasting as long as his orgasm, squeezed out between his lips and teeth. She fell forward into him, weakened, and the change of angle where they were still joined—where he was still so sensitive—caused a full-body jerk in his and the oath finally spilled across his talented lips, loud and crude.

And almost holy.

'Potty mouth,' she gasped against his sweat-dampened ear when she could eventually re-coordinate the passage of air in and out of her lungs.

His breath came in heaves and he swallowed several times before finally making words. 'I have no dignity with you.'

A place deep inside her chest squeezed as hard as the muscles between her legs just had.

*...with you.*

But she'd been protecting herself for too long to indulge the pleasure for more than a moment before she bundled the thought down where all the others milled, unvoiced, and focused instead on the decadent honey slugging through her veins and the punishing tenderness of flesh she'd finally used as nature intended.

'My God.'

Such simple words but there was something in them, something super powerful in the fact that she almost never invoked the 'g' word. But it belonged here with them today. Because what had just happened between them was as reverential as anything she could imagine.

She twisted sideways and squeezed down next to Oliver as he shuffled over in the big chair, both of them taking a moment to right themselves and their underwear.

*Undignified*, he had said and he wasn't wrong, but, strangely, dignity had no place here tonight. Neither of them required it and neither of them mourned its absence. Audrey curled into his still heaving body.

'Thank you,' she breathed and felt more than saw the questioning tilt of his head. 'You're very good at this.'

Tension drummed its fingers everywhere their bodies met. Odd, considering she'd given him a compliment.

'We're good *together*,' he clarified.

Her own throaty chuckle was positively indecent. 'I could learn so much from you.'

It was hard to know whether his resulting silence was discomfort at the suggestion of a future between them or something else. But his tone, when he eventually spoke, wasn't harsh.

'I'm like a theme-park ride to you, aren't I?'

'Best ever.'

Fastest, highest, most thrilling. And most unforgettable.

His smile was immediate, but there was an indefinably sad quality to the sigh just before he spoke. 'Come on. Let's move back to the lounge. Will your legs work?'

The idea of stretching out with Oliver as they had earlier, of falling asleep in his arms, was too tempting. She practically rolled off the chair. 'If they won't, I'll crawl.'

Nope. Not one shred of dignity. But when they had so little time together, and when she might well not see him again for twelve months—or at all—really what did it matter?

It was his pedestal, not hers.

She might as well throw herself off it before she tumbled off.

# CHAPTER ELEVEN

*Salted caramel chocolate ice cream topped with gold leaf*

'AUDREY DEVANEY, YOU are such a paradox,' Oliver murmured from his position sitting knees up on the floor beside the sofa a deeply unconscious woman was presently stretched out on. He stroked a strand of dark hair away from her sleep-relaxed mouth.

That mouth.

The one he wanted to go on kissing forever. The one he'd pretty much given up hope of ever getting closer than a civil, social air-kiss to.

The one he'd bruised with his epic hours of worship.

She was like a wild creature released from captivity. Joyous and curious and adventurous yet heartbreakingly cautious. Running wild, tonight, in her attempt to experience everything she'd missed in life.

She was gorging on new experience. They both were.

But just for different reasons.

For Audrey…? She *was* on a theme park ride. The sort of thing you only did once a year but you had a blast while you were doing it. Whatever she lacked in experience, she made up double in raw enthusiasm and natural aptitude.

And for him…?

He knew that the moment she walked out of that door, this amazing woman would be lost to him. Away from the hypnotic chemistry that pulsed between them, her clever mind would start rationalising their night together, her doubts would skitter back to the fore, her busy life and her old-school common sense would have her filing their hours together away as some kind of treasure to be brought out and remembered fondly. Hotly, if he was any judge.

But very definitely in the past.

He traced the fine line of her cool arm with a fingertip.

And that was probably all for the better given he had no kind of future to offer her and she was absolutely not the booty-call type. If he were another kind of man he would happily spend eternity sharing her interests, respecting and trusting her. All the things she valued in a relationship.

If he were that man.

But he wasn't. He'd proposed to Tiffany because he was tired and she was there, and because she was the kind of woman who would have cheated on him long before he could ever cheat on her. *When, not if.*

Because genes would out. His inability to find a woman he could stick to was proof positive.

*That* was the kind of man he was.

He sure as hell wasn't the kind who could be trusted with what he'd seen in Audrey's eyes back on that chair. The look she was too overwhelmed to disguise. Or deny. The unveiled look just before she shattered into a hundred pieces in his lap. That was not the look of a woman for whom this wasn't a big deal. It was not the look that belonged with the words she was saying.

It was a glimpse of the real Audrey.

And of what he really wanted. What he never knew, until tonight, *that* he wanted.

And what he damn well knew he couldn't have.

Tonight, he got a glimpse of something deeper than just sexy or smart or unattainable. Something much more fundamental.

Audrey's soul communicating directly with his.

That moment when it crashed headlong into his and its eyes flared with surprise and it whispered, incredulously, *Oh, that's right. There you are.*

He wasn't prepared to even put a name to the sensation. Not when a candle could burn longer than the time they had left together. Walking away tomorrow—today, really—was going to hurt her. But short-term pain had to be better than a lifetime of it, right?

But he was weak enough and selfish enough that he wanted to be the man against whom *she* measured all others. He wanted a place in her heart that nothing and no one could touch. Not some future man, not some future experience. A place she would smile and ache when she accessed it, the way he did with his memories of her. The smiles and the aches that sustained him through the year between her visits.

The bittersweet memories that would sustain him through his whole damn life.

And so, as ridiculous and pointless as it probably was, he wasn't letting her out of his sight until the law said he had to. He was going to keep her with him until morning, he was going to drive her back to her hotel and then deliver her to the airport and even the flight gate, personally. He was going to pour everything he wanted to say to her but couldn't into their last hours together and he was going to show her the kind of night a woman would find impossible to forget.

Because if he wasn't going to have her in his life he would damn well make sure he endured in her memory. Haunted it like some sad, desperate spectre. Made an impression on her heart.

A dent.

Hell, he'd take a scratch. She'd spent so long protecting it he wouldn't be surprised to find her heart was plated in three-inch steel. That was what would get her through the disappointment of them parting in seven hours.

Audrey murmured and resettled in her sleep, her fingers coming up to brush her lips as if feeling the memory of his kiss. A tiny frown marred her perfect skin.

But he was no masochist. He would take these last hours before Audrey climbed on her plane in the knowledge that, quite possibly, it was all she was ever going to give him. And he'd keep her close and make it special and live off the memories of it forever.

Too many parts of him needed this night too badly not to.

'Wakey-wakey, beautiful.'

Audrey's lashes fluttered open and it took a moment for her to orient herself against the odd sight that filled her field of vision. It looked like a giant tongue, curled back onto itself and with an ornate, gold insect perched on the top.

'Did a dragonfly escape?' Actually, there were two of them. The first one's twin sat on a matching dish across the table. Really, really spectacular escapees.

'Final course,' Oliver murmured from somewhere behind her.

She lifted her head and the world righted. She was stretched out on the sofa where they'd moved, exhausted, with Oliver's coat draped modestly over her bare legs.

She struggled into a sitting position, wriggling her skirt back down. 'I thought everyone had gone?' She hoped to heaven that was true and no one was in the kitchen while they got all Kama Sutra on the armchair.

'Looks like they didn't want us to miss out on the pièce de résistance. I found it in the kitchen cold room with a note on it saying "eat me".'

Well, that was about perfect for this whole Alice in Wonderland evening. If she grew until she banged her head on

Qīngtíng's ornate ceiling she couldn't have felt more transformed than she did by the night's events.

Emotionally, spiritually.

She was leaving Hong Kong a changed woman.

She swung her legs off the sofa and blinked a few times to regain full consciousness. 'What time is it?'

'Half past five.'

*A.M.?* They'd lost precious hours to sleeping. She twisted to look behind her. Oliver knelt behind the sofa, his chin resting on the beautifully embroidered back. He looked as if he'd been there a while. He also looked extremely content.

And extremely gorgeous.

The cold, hard light of morning sat awkwardly on her, though. Flashes of how she'd behaved over by the window. The Audrey she'd never suspected was in there. The Audrey only Oliver could have freed.

'What have you been doing?'

'Just watching you sleep.'

She frowned and scrubbed at gritty eyes before remembering the face full of make-up she was probably no longer wearing. Her fists dropped. 'Stalker.'

His soft laugh caressed her in places she'd never felt a laugh before. 'I didn't do it the whole time. I've made a few calls, cleaned the kitchen up a bit—'

Presumably how he'd found the ice cream...

'—and sorted us for breakfast.'

He'd made calls? Done business while she was in a sex-induced coma?

*Way to strip the special from something there, Oliver.* 'Do you not need sleep?'

'I have the rest of the year to sleep.'

Elation tangled in her chest with disappointment. On one hand, that was tantamount to saying he also didn't want to miss a moment of their day. On the other hand, it said she was definitely getting on that flight at ten this morning.

Had she imagined last night would change anything? He'd made her no promises. If anything he'd forced her to verbalise what they both knew. That this was a time-limited, once-in-a-lifetime offer. No coupon required. She'd gone out of her way not to look too closely at *why* it was happening. She'd just thrilled at the fact it was happening and let the fantasy get away with her. Let herself be whoever she wanted to be.

And last night she'd wanted to be *that* woman. The one who could keep up with a man like Oliver and walk away, head high in the morning.

Regardless of how she felt inside.

And if nothing else Audrey Devaney was a woman who always—always—made the beds she'd lain in. And so she did what always worked for her in moments of crisis—especially at five-thirty a.m.

She ignored it.

She picked up one of the plated dark tongues instead. 'What is this?'

'Chocolate caramel ice cream.'

An understatement if the rest of the evening's astonishments were anything to go by. This was bound to be so much more than just ice cream. 'Why is there a dragonfly on it?'

'It's gold leaf. Qīngtíng's signature dish.'

She peered at the extraordinary craftsmanship. An intricate and beautiful dragonfly perfectly rendered in real gold leaf. No wonder the chef hadn't wanted them to miss it.

'I don't know whether to eat it or frame it,' she breathed, after a long study.

'Eat it. I suspect it's too fine to last long.'

Eating gold. That was going to take a little getting used to. Just like the sudden intimacy in Oliver's gravelly voice. He moved across from her, sat on *her* sofa, and watched her as she sliced her splade down across the back of the decorative insect and took a chunk out of the perfect curl of ice cream.

Salty, caramely, chocolaty goodness teased her senses into full consciousness.

'This is sublime.' Then something occurred to her. 'Is this breakfast?'

Why the heck not when the rest of the past twenty-four hours was Lewis Carroll kind of surreal? Ice cream and gold for breakfast fitted right in.

'This is the end of dinner. Breakfast will be in about ninety minutes.'

Breakfast meant sunrise. And sunrise meant it was time to go back to the real world. Audrey was suddenly suffused with a chill that had nothing to do with the delicious creamy dessert. She laid the splade across her barely touched dish.

'How long before dawn?'

His eyes narrowed. 'Sun-up is at six fifty-eight a.m.'

'That's very precise.'

'It's the winter solstice. A big deal in China.'

Right. Not like he'd been counting the minutes. 'What will we do until then?'

'Why, what happens at daybreak? You planning on doing a Cinderella on me?'

Did he know how close he was to the truth?

'As it happens you won't be able to,' he went on. 'We're going to be somewhere special at sunrise. Somewhere you'd struggle to run away from.'

The most special place she could imagine being as the sun crept over Hong Kong's mountains was back upstairs in that big, comfortable bed wrapped in Oliver's arms and both of them sleeping right through breakfast in satiated slumber.

A girl could dream.

'Sounds intriguing,' she said past the ache in her heart.

'I hope so. I had to pull a few strings to make it happen.'

Was he throwing a bunch of people out of another restaurant? 'You're not going to tell me?'

'No. I'd like it to be a surprise. Though I should ask… Can you swim?'

It was a necessary question.

Forty minutes later, Audrey stood on the pier at Tsim Sha Tsui staring at a gracious, fully restored Chinese junk.

'I've seen this at night going up and down the harbour,' she breathed, walking the boat's moored length, running her hand along the one-hundred-and-fifty-year-old dark hull timbers. Its bright-red sails were usually illuminated by uplights and seemed to those on shore to glow red fire as it drifted silently across the water. This morning, though, no glowing sails, just a network of pretty oriental lanterns throwing a gentle light across the deck cluttered with boating business but devoid of any people.

'That's our sunrise ride.'

She was glad she was still in her silk dress for this, but she was also glad for the drape of Oliver's coat around her shoulders. As soon as she'd stepped out of the car he'd arranged for the slow drive to the Kowloon pier, the cool bite of morning had made itself known. But she tried to keep her appreciation purely functional and not fixate on the smell and warmth of gorgeous man as it soaked into her skin.

On board, they passed the first quarter-hour exploring the rigging and construction of the small junk and appreciating the three-hundred-and-sixty-degree views and the sounds of the waking harbour. But as the sky lightened and the vessel swung in a big arc to drift back up the waterfront again Oliver moved them to the upper deck, really the old roof of the covered lower deck, and propped them up against the mast of the fully unfurled centre sail.

A basket appeared courtesy of a fleet-footed, bowing crewman, filled to overflowing with fresh fruits and gorgeous pastries with a thermos of fragrant coffee. Oliver pressed his back to the mast, then pulled Audrey into the V of his legs and, between them, they picked the delicious contents of the basket clean as the sun rose over the mountainous islands of Hong Kong. The fiery orb first turned the harbour and everything around it a shimmering silver and then a rich gold before finally settling on a soft-focus blue.

The sounds of traditional oriental music drifted across the harbour as they passed a group of workers doing dawn t'ai chi by the water.

'What do you think?' he murmured.

The canvas above them issued an almost inaudible hum as it vibrated under the strain of the morning breeze. The same breeze that gave them motion. 'I think it's spectacular. I've always wanted to sail on this boat.' She twisted more towards him. 'Thank you.'

His lips fell on hers so naturally. Lingered. 'You're welcome.'

Yet it wasn't the same as the many—many—kisses they'd shared tonight because it wasn't really *tonight* at all. It was now *today.* And it was daylight and the real world was waking around them—solstice or not—and getting on with their lives.

Which was what they needed to do.

They'd been doing the whole *make-believe* for long enough.

'You've sure raised the bar on first dates,' she breathed without thinking, but then caught herself. 'I mean…any date.'

Discomfort radiated through his body and into hers. 'It's a kind of first date.'

No, it wasn't. The awkward tension in his voice was a dead giveaway.

'First implies there'll be more,' she said, critically light. 'We're more of an *only* date, really.'

And, importantly, it was the *end* of the only date. After breakfast she really needed to be thinking about picking up her stuff from the hotel and getting out to the airport over on Lantau. Before she made more of a fool of herself than she already had.

Before she curled her fingers around his strong arms and refused, point-blank, to let go.

'You don't see there being more?'

It was impossible to know what his casual question was hoping to ferret out. A yes or a no. It was veiled enough to be either.

Every part of her tightened but she kept her voice light. Determined to be modern and grown-up about this. 'We live in different countries, Oliver. That makes future dates a bit hard, doesn't it?'

'What we live in is a technological age. There are dozens of ways for us to stay connected.'

Not physically. And that was what he was talking about, right? Even though she got the sense he was speaking against his own will. 'I'm not sure I'm really the sexting type.'

*Huh.* She all but felt it in the puff of breath on the back of her neck.

'So…that's it? One night of wild sex and you're done?'

She twisted in his arms and locked her eyes on his. 'What were you hoping for, two nights? Three?' She held his gaze and challenged him. 'More?'

His face grew intensely guarded.

*Yeah. Just as she thought.*

'We have until ten,' he reminded her.

'What difference will a few more hours make?'

'Look what a difference the first few made.'

True enough. Her life had turned on its head in less than twelve hours. 'But what difference will it *make*? Really?'

Heat blazed down on her. 'I didn't expect you to be scrabbling to get away from me.'

She sat up straighter, pulled away a few precious inches. 'I'm not scrabbling, Oliver. I'm just being realistic.'

'Can't you be realistic on the way to the airport?'

She studied him closely. His face gave nothing away. Again, part of his success in the corporate world. 'Right down to the wire?'

'I just… This haste is unsettling.'

'You've never tiptoed out of a hotel room at dawn before?'

'Yeah I have, and I know what that means. So I don't like you doing it to me.'

'Oh.' She shifted away and curled her legs more under her. 'You don't like being revealed as a hypocrite.'

'Is it hypocrisy to have enjoyed our night together and not want it to end?'

'It has to end,' she pointed out. But then she couldn't help herself. Maybe he knew something she didn't. 'Doesn't it?'

If he clenched his jaw any tighter it was going to fracture. 'Yeah, it does.'

'Yeah,' she repeated. 'It does.' Because they were only ever going to be a one-off thing. A question answered. An itch scratched. 'Sydney's waiting for me. Shanghai's waiting for you.'

Except of course that he was on the phone this morning making up for time lost to their…adventures. So, Shanghai didn't really need to wait all that long at all, did it?

Was the morning after always this awkward? She could totally understand why he might have snuck out in the past to avoid it.

'Did you make plans for the next few hours?' she tested.

'I did.'

'And you didn't want to run them past me, first? What if I had Testore business this morning?'

Okay, now they just sounded like a bickering couple. But the line between generous and controlling wasn't all that thick. And bickering gave all the simmering pain somewhere to go.

He had enough grace to flush. 'Do you?'

She let out a long, slow breath. Maybe it would be smarter to say yes. To get off this boat and hurry off to some imaginary appointment. But he'd done this lovely thing... 'No. I took care of it all earlier in the week.'

He nodded. Then sagged. 'It was supposed to be the perfect end to the—' he bit back his own words and straightened '—to a nice night.'

*Nice.* Ouch.

'We're on a one-hundred-and-fifty-year-old private junk on Victoria Harbour at sunrise on the winter solstice. You've done well, Oliver.'

He stared out at a ferry that rumbled past them. Its wake slapped against the junk's hull like lame applause. He sighed. 'So, you want to head back in?'

She probably should.

'I don't want this to end any sooner than it has to.' She caught and held his gaze despite the ache deep in her chest. 'But I do respect that it does have to.'

Denial was one thing... Delusion was just foolish.

She settled back against his legs. 'We'll head back when we're due.'

It took him a while to relax behind her, but she felt the moment he accepted her words. His body softened, his hand crept up to gather her wind-whipped hair into a protected ponytail that he gently stroked in time with the sloshing of the waves. She sank back into his caress.

As if she'd been doing it always.

As if she always would.

Her friend. With shiny, new, short-term benefits.

Maybe that was just what they'd be now. Not that he'd

offered anything other than a vague and unplanned cyber 'more'. She tried to imagine dropping into Shanghai for a quickie whenever she was in Asia and just couldn't. That wasn't her. Despite all evidence to the contrary, overnight. Despite the woman she'd seen reflected in the dragonfly terrarium.

Which was not to say her body wasn't *screaming* at her to be that person, but last night was really about years of longing finally being fulfilled. And it was all about fairy tales and chemistry and the loudly ticking approach of dawn. It had nothing to do with reality. Living together day to day, or the occasional fight, or morning breath or blanket hogging, or making the mortgage or any of the many unromantic things that made up a relationship.

It was what it was. A magical storybook ending to an unconventional friendship.

More than magical, really. It was dream-come-true country.

And everyone knew that anything that seemed too good to be true…probably was. But she'd take it while it was on offer—including the next few hours—because she was unlikely to see its equal again in her life.

Ever.

# CHAPTER TWELVE

*Sulewesi coffee beans with eggnog and nutmeg*

COLLECTING AUDREY'S THINGS and checking out of her hotel room while most people were still asleep took an easy fifteen minutes and then they were back in the limo and heading out to Stanley on the southern-most tip of Hong Kong island. Within the half-hour Oliver was pulling back a chair for her on the balcony of a one-hundred-and-seventy-year-old colonial hotel with views of the South China Sea stretching out forever, and with the single morning waiter much relieved they were only there for coffee.

Albeit a pricey coffee from one of the most exclusive plantations on the planet.

Audrey smiled at him—pretty, but each one getting progressively emptier as the morning wore on. As though she were already on that jet flying away from him.

'Eggnog, Oliver? At eight in the morning?'

'Eggnog *coffee*. And it's Christmas.'

And he wanted to spring into her mind whenever she smelled cinnamon. Or a coffee bean. Or the ocean.

'Can I ask you something?' she said after stirring hers for an age.

He lifted his eyes.

'Is this hard for you?'

Her clear, direct eyes said *be honest* and so he was. Or

as honest as he knew how to be, anyway. 'You leaving in a few hours?'

'All of it. Knowing what to do. Knowing how to deal with it. Or is this just par for the course in your life?'

He took a deep breath. Whatever he said now would set the tone for how the rest of the morning went. How they parted. As friends or something less. Carelessness now could really hurt her. 'You think that last night happens for me all the time?'

'It might.'

'It doesn't.'

'What was different?'

He fought to keep his expression more relaxed than the rest of his tight body would allow. 'Fishing for compliments?'

His cowardice caused a flush of heat in her alabaster cheeks. Of course she wasn't. She was Audrey.

'I don't know how to go back from here, Oliver. And I know that we can't go forward.'

'Depends on how you define forward.'

'I define it as progress. Improvement.' She took a breath. 'More.'

A rock the size of his fist pressed against the bottom of his gut. *Forward* just opened up too much opportunity for hurt for her. This was Audrey. With all kinds of strength yet as fragile as the gold leaf they'd eaten back at the restaurant. She deserved much better than a man who had no ability to commit.

He wasn't about to risk her heart on a bad investment. On *more.*

'Then no. We can't go forward.'

Those enormous, all-seeing eyes scrutinised him but gave nothing away. 'Yet we can't go back.'

'We're still friends.'

'With benefits?'

'With or without. I'll always count you as a friend, Audrey. And I don't have many of those.'

'That's because you don't trust anyone.'

'I trust you.'

Her eyes reflected the azure around them. As crisp and sharp as a knife.

'Why do you?'

'Because you've never lied to me. I'd know if you did.'

'You think so? Maybe I'm just really good at it.' Because she'd been lying for eight years denying the attraction she felt for him and he'd missed that. 'So, do I see you more or less in the coming year? What's the plan?'

Less than once? Was she talking about not coming next Christmas? A deep kind of panic took hold of his gut and twisted. The same agony he'd felt last year when she didn't show. He struggled against it.

'What makes you think I have a plan?'

'Because you're you. And because you had hours while I was sleeping to come up with one.'

He shrugged, a postcard for nonchalance. 'You weren't interested in sexting.'

How could she find it in herself to laugh while he was so tight inside? Even if it was the emptiest he'd ever heard from her. 'I'm still not.' She locked eyes with his. 'So am I right to sleep with other men, then?'

The blood decamped from his face so fast it left him dizzy. 'I didn't realise there was a queue.'

She leaned onto her elbows on the table. 'Just trying to get my parameters. Will you be sleeping with anyone?'

'Audrey…'

'Because Christmas is a long time off.'

Wow, he was like a yo-yo around her. Excited now that Christmas—a Christmas that might include both of them— was back on the radar. But the roller coaster only decreased his control of this situation.

'Warming to your newfound sexuality?'

Her eyes finally grew as flat and lifeless as he feared they would around him. 'Yes, Oliver. I want to give it a good workout with anyone I meet. Maybe even the waiter.'

He stared her down. 'Sarcasm does not become you.'

She lifted both brows.

'What the hell do you want from me, Audrey?'

'I want you to say it out loud.'

'Say what?'

'That this is it. That there is no more. I need to hear it in your voice. I need to see the words forming on your lips.'

There wasn't enough air to speak. So he just stared.

'Because otherwise I will wait for you. I'll hold this amazing memory close to my heart and, even though I won't want it to, it will stop me forming new relationships because I'll always be secretly hoping that you're going to change your mind. And call. Or drop by. Or send me air tickets. And I'll want to be free for that.

'So you need to tell me now, Oliver. For real and for certain. So there is no doubt.' She took the deepest breath her twisted chest could manage. 'Should I be planning to spend any more time with you this year?'

'Have I offered you a future?'

A punch below her diaphragm couldn't have been more effective. But it didn't matter that she couldn't answer, because Oliver's question was rhetorical.

They both knew the answer.

'I don't do relationships, Audrey. I do great, short, blazing affairs. Like last night. And I do long hours at the office and constant travel. My driver sees more of me than most of my girlfriends do.'

Did he use the present tense on purpose?

'But I'm the woman against whom you measure others.'

The words that had been so romantic last night sounded ludicrous in the cold, hard light of rejection.

'You are. You always will be.'

'But that's still not enough to pierce your heart?'

'What do hearts have to do with anything? I respect you and I care for you. Too much to risk—'

'To risk what?'

'To risk you. To risk hurting you more than I already have.'

'Shouldn't that have been something you thought of before you let things get hot and heavy between us? Do you imagine this doesn't hurt?'

Shame flitted behind his eyes. 'You knew the score.'

'Yes, I did. And I went ahead anyway.' More fool her. 'But something changed in me in that stupid armchair this morning. I realised that one day every eight years is not enough for me. I realised I *am* good enough for you. I am just as valuable and worthy and beautiful as any of the other women in your life. And most importantly I am not broken.'

He didn't respond, and the old Audrey crept back in for a half-heartbeat. 'Unless you're a much better liar than I believed?'

No. You couldn't fake the facial contortions and guttural declarations Oliver had made. They were real.

A fierce conviction suffused his face. 'You are not broken.'

'So how do you feel that some other man is going to enjoy the benefits of your…training? How will you feel when you imagine me with my thighs wrapped around a stranger instead of you? When I let someone other than you deep inside me? When I choke on someone else's name?'

His nostrils flared and he gritted words out. 'Not great. But you're not mine to keep.'

'I could be.' All he had to say was 'stay'.

'No.'

'Why?'

'Because I don't want you to be mine.'

*I don't want you.* Something ruptured and flapped wildly deep in her chest. 'You wanted me last night.'

'And now I've had you.'

Her stomach plunged. Was that it? Question answered? Itch scratched? Challenge conquered? 'No. I don't believe you. You respect me too much.'

'You were a goddess, Audrey. Chaste and unattainable.'

And now she was what…? Fallen? But then something sank through the painful misery clogging her sense. One word. A word she'd used herself. On herself.

*Unattainable.*

And she realised.

'You thought I was safe.'

His eyes shifted out to sea.

'You thought I was someone you could just quietly obsess on without ever having to risk being called on it. Someone to hang this ideal of perfection on and excuse your inability to commit to anyone else, but utterly, utterly safe. First I was married and you could hide behind a ring and your own values. Then you thought I wasn't interested in that kind of relationship with you and so you just got to brood about it like some modern-day Heathcliff, torturing yourself with my presence once a year.'

Something on the distant horizon sure had his focus…

'But what's a man to do when the woman he's been wanting for so long throws herself at you? You broke your own rule.'

His gaze snapped back to hers. 'I should have been stronger. You were vulnerable.'

'Oh, please, I think we've established that there is no pedestal strong enough to take me and all my foibles. I was pissed off but I wasn't vulnerable. I knew exactly what I

was putting my hand up for. And you made a move long before you told me about Blake. So it was hardly reactionary.'

'It was weak.'

'Damn straight it was. And it still is if you're unwilling
to just say "it's been fun, but it's over".'

'That's what you want?'

'That's what I need if I'm not to spend the next twelve
months suffering death by a thousand cuts. Because if you
don't say it—*and mean it*—I won't believe it. I know myself too well.'

He marshalled himself visibly. 'It *was* fun, Audrey. And
it *is* over. Last night was a one-time thing. And it's not because of any lack on your part or because it didn't measure
up compared to anyone else. It's because that's how I roll.
I don't do relationships and nothing and no one can really
change a man's nature.'

'Not even a paragon?'

He shuddered a deep breath and his voice gentled. 'Not
even a paragon.'

'So what will you do for the rest of your life? Be alone?'

'I'll find another Tiffany.'

'Someone to *settle* for?'

'Someone I can't hurt.'

What did that *mean*? 'You think the Tiffanys of this
world don't have feelings?'

'She was as hard as I am.'

That stopped her in her tracks. 'Why do you think you're
hard?'

'Because I can't—' But he wouldn't let himself finish
that sentence.

*Love?* Was that what he'd refused to say aloud? Well,
she wasn't about to be the first. 'You think you *can't* be
in a relationship just because you *haven't* been in a successful one?'

'I'm not afraid to acknowledge my weaknesses, Audrey. I just don't do commitment.'

She sat back hard into her bamboo-woven chair. 'What if it's weakness not to even try?'

Two lines cut deep between his eyebrows. 'It's not just about me. It's not some lab experiment or computer formula. There's another person there. A living breathing feeling person existing in a marriage that's not healthy for them.'

Marriage? Wait… How had they got there?

'But it's okay if she's…hard?' she said. Wasn't that the word he'd used?

'If she knows the score. Accepts it.'

'Accepts what?'

'The limitations of the relationship.'

'Oliver, I really don't understand—'

'Do the maths, Audrey,' he grated. 'You're a smart woman.'

She was, but clearly not in this. 'Are you talking about a relationship without commitment?'

'Commitment *traps*.'

She flopped back into her chair. 'Who? You?'

'Her.'

Wait… 'Is this about your mother?'

'She was trapped with a worthless human being because of her feelings for him.'

'She made a conscious choice to stay, Oliver.'

'There was no choice. Not back then.'

Did he fear love because he'd seen his mother suffer at the hands of an unfaithful husband? 'I can't imagine her being a weak woman.'

He blinked at her. 'What? No.'

'Then she made her own choices. Informed choices. She stayed because she wanted to. Or she decided he was worth it.'

'If not for me she could have walked. Should have.'

Did he hear his own Freudian slip? He blamed his mother for toughing it out with a serial cheater. 'It was the eighties, Oliver, not the fifties. She could have left him, even with a child in tow. Plenty of women did.'

'She wanted me to have a father.'

'Then that was her conscious decision. And it was a noble one. She loved him. And you.'

There. She said it aloud. The L word.

'Love trapped her.'

There was that word again. Maybe it wasn't about the love, maybe it was about the trapping.

'So, this is about your father?'

'If she'd cared as little as he obviously did the whole thing wouldn't have hurt her so much.'

*Someone I can't hurt.*

Oh.

A wash of dreadful awareness pooled in her aching chest and gut. She had to force the words across her lips. 'You don't want to repeat your parents' marriage. Where one person has feelings the other doesn't.'

This was his way of telling her he didn't—couldn't—love her. And this was why another Tiffany was a better bet for him.

'I don't ever want you to feel the way she felt.'

Trapped. In a one-sided relationship.

'You assume it would be that way.'

'I know myself.'

He meant he knew his feelings. But she was desperate enough to push. 'So you just avoid any kind of commitment just in case? What if I'm the exception?'

'You deserve someone who can be everything you are.'

'Yet, apparently, this paragon is still not worthy. Except for a bit of wham-bam-thank-you-ma'am.'

'You're the best person I know,' he muttered.

*Oh, please...* 'You just defiled the best person you know. I'd hate to see how you treat everyone else.'

She pushed her half-finished coffee away and stumbled to her feet. Correction, half-drunk but most definitely finished.

Like this relationship.

'This is what's going to happen now,' she began, working hard to keep the thick clag of pain from her voice. 'You are going to call your car around and tell him to take me to the airport. We will drop you back at your hotel on the way and all of this will be a surreal memory by morning.'

She omitted the part about her crying all the way back to Australia and never having another relationship again in her life. That didn't seem conducive to a dignified exit.

'I'm coming to the airport...'

She stopped and glared at him. 'Because this isn't hard enough?'

'Because it's over for me, then, too. I need to see you walking away.'

'Why, Oliver? Why not just let me go? Do the right thing.'

'I'm already doing the right thing. One day I hope you'll believe that.'

She knew she could hold it all together back to the harbour, but could she do it all the way over to Lantau? And then waiting for her flight to board?

She turned from him and walked towards the stairs, not even sure she could hold it together as far as the top tread. Behind her, he murmured into his phone, and as her foot touched the last flight, the limo pulled up outside the charming old building.

She crawled in without a word.

Oliver followed.

They sat as far apart as the spacious back seat would allow.

All the way back to Central Hong Kong Audrey peered out of the window at the complicated mix of green, verdant hills and dense, crowded, multicultural residential areas. Chances were good she'd be back in Hong Kong on a future instrument hunt but she knew she'd only ever have flying visits. This was no longer a place of pleasure.

It was now wrecked.

She swallowed past the thick lump resident in her throat.

As they approached the Western Harbour tunnel over to Kowloon and Mainland China she glanced east and saw the same junk they'd breakfasted on puttering between bigger vessels in the busy harbour, her sails ablaze. Filled with other people who would imagine it as *their* special thing. Only to discover it wasn't special at all.

Just like this whole experience.

Perhaps she'd projected too much of her own feelings onto Oliver. Perhaps she'd been foolish to indulge them after they'd come back down to the restaurant. *She'd* reignited things between them then, not him. She had to own that. She'd thought she was capable of handling a one-night stand but that was when it was *circumstance* keeping them apart, not some ill-defined deficiency on her part.

Whatever it was that meant Oliver couldn't imagine himself loving her as much as she—

Across the car, he seemed to flinch as though he could hear her thoughts and knew what was going to come next.

*—loved him.*

Her stomach plunged and she blamed the tunnel that sank deeper under Victoria Harbour. There really was no question: she'd adored Oliver Harmer for years. The only mystery was when, exactly, it had graduated into love. Her body had recognised it in the wee hours of this morning, when his hands were in her hair and he was buried deep in her and his eyes blazed up at her in a way that was so close to *worship*...

She didn't have any experience in what love looked like but she'd felt so certain that it looked just like that. That moment where her soul and his connected. Her subconscious had named it even if she hadn't.

But what would she know?

Maybe he always looked like that when he came?

What if she was exactly as ill equipped to be with a man like Oliver as she'd always feared? What if the whole night had just been one big try-hard exercise on her part and he was just trying to extract himself from an uncomfortable situation?

What if she'd overreached after all?

The tears she'd done such a good job of holding back refused to let that last thought go unanswered. They spilled silently over her lids, along her lashes and then down her cheeks. She let them run, only the tunnel walls to witness.

But the spill became a river and the river a trembling torrent, and as they surfaced out of the tunnel and merged onto Highway 5 she couldn't disguise what was happening any longer.

'Audrey—'

Her hand shot up in warning to him as her body doubled over at the combined pain of his rejection and the humiliation of this moment. Only the glass of her window stopped her from crumpling right over and she pressed her forehead against its cool reassurance.

The minute strength she had left was in her silence and so she still didn't give the slightest voice to the sorrow.

'Audrey…'

No. Not compassion, not from Oliver. She struggled against him when he moved closer and slid one arm around her shoulders, but her pathetic resistance was no match for his gentle strength.

'Shh…'

He pulled her against his chest, into his arms and just

held her. No platitudes. No promises. No lies. Just silent compassion.

And that made it all so much worse.

She was losing the man she loved and her best friend all at the same time.

The last of her resilience gave way on a hoarse, horrible sob and she buried her shame into his chest. She cried as they passed Stonecutter's Island. She cried as they crossed onto Tsing Yi. She cried as they rose on a suspension bridge high above the water and breached the two-kilometre ocean passage to Lantau. She cried right past the turnoff to the most magical theme park in China and she cried the full length of Highway 8.

And the whole time, Oliver just stroked her hair, fed her tissues and held her.

For the last time, ever.

A voice crackled on the intercom and she recognised the name of Hong Kong's primary airport. That and the interrupting voice was enough to lurch her up out of Oliver's gentle hold and back to her far corner where she pressed a series of fresh, folded tissues to her stinging, swollen eyes.

And still Oliver didn't speak.

What was there to say?

She'd just melted down on him for the second time in twenty-four hours. He'd already said he didn't know what to do with her when she was like this. And Hong Kong's traffic meant it was a long ride with a hysterical woman.

*Tough luck, buddy. This one's all on you.* This was his decision. This was his issue.

'I don't want you to come in,' she gritted between pats. 'At the airport.'

'I need to see you to your gate.'

To make sure she actually left? She half turned her head to beg him, 'And I'm asking you to do what *I* need, not what *you* need.'

His silent stare bored into the back of her head. 'Okay, Audrey.'

'Thank you.'

The limo negotiated the tangle of taxis, buses and private cars clogging the airport's approach until it began moving up the causeway. That seemed to press Oliver into action at last.

'Don't you think it would be easier for me to just go with the flow,' he bit out. 'To just say "see you in Sydney" and to swing by when I'm in town for a hot hook-up? I didn't want to be that man.'

That brought Audrey's gaze back around to his. 'Should I applaud?'

'I'd like you to understand. My motives if not my reasons.'

'You're avoiding commitment. Seems patently clear.'

He exhaled on a hiss. 'I'm avoiding—' He cut his own words off. 'I didn't want to hurt you, Audrey. I *don't* want to. I'm sorry, but, as bad as we both feel, ultimately it will be better this way.'

'You have nothing to apologise for, Oliver. You've lived up to your reputation and given me a night I will never forget. For so many reasons.' Her smile was tight. 'I get it, I really do.'

'Do you?'

'I'm going to go back to Sydney, throw myself into my work and concentrate on low-hanging fruit from now on.' That was a lie, she wasn't going to be interested in fruit of any kind for a long, long time.

'Audrey, don't do that to yourself. This is about me, not you.'

He seemed to wince at the triteness of his own words.

'You're right. This is about you and your inability to let go of the past. This is about you being so afraid that you'll end up like your father you're avoiding any kind of commitment at all. You dress it up in chivalry and concern for me, but, let's be honest, this is all about you.'

His eyes grew as hard as his clenched jaw.

The limo pulled up to the concourse and Audrey had her door open practically before it had stopped. Oliver leapt out after her as the driver came around to the rear for her case.

'I've held a candle for you since I met you, Oliver. You were everything that I wanted and believed I didn't deserve. You came to be symbolic in my life of my own deficiencies and I wore them like a badge of shame.

'But you know what? I *don't* deserve the man you are. You are the one that doesn't measure up, Oliver Harmer. You are so fixated on not being the serial cheat your father was, you can't see that you've become exactly like him, ravaging from woman to woman spreading the misery around.

'Well, I'm done doubting myself.' She poked his chest. 'I'm awesome. And clever. And pretty. And loyal.' Every poke an accusation. 'And the best friend a person could have. I would have been fierce and proud by your side and someone you could face life with, head-on. But that honour is going to go to someone else and I'm not going to be able to find him while you're still in my life.'

She let her expressive hands drop by her sides. As dead as she felt. 'So this is it, Oliver. After eight years. No more card games, no more conversations, no more long, lazy lunches that you can cling to in lieu of a real relationship with a real woman.' Her shoulders shuddered up and then dropped. 'No more Christmas. If I'm not in your life then I'm out of it. You don't get to have it both ways.' She settled her bag more firmly between them. 'Please don't email me. Or call. Don't send me a birthday card. Don't invite me to your wedding with whichever Tiffany you find next.'

Fortunately, she'd used up all her tears coming across the causeway. Oliver wasn't so lucky and the glitter of those hazel eyes just about broke her heart anew.

Audrey swung her bag around, smiled her thanks to the driver trying so very hard not to listen, and then forced her eyes back onto Oliver before whispering tightly, 'But I *beg* you not to settle for a loveless life. That is not what your mother sacrificed her life to teach you.'

And then she turned and he was gone from her vision. From her life.

But never, ever, ever from her heart.

# CHAPTER THIRTEEN

*December 20th, this year*

THE PERFECT, PRACTISED English washed over him as Oliver stared out across Victoria Harbour at the building that housed Qīngtíng and the penthouse at its very top, absently rolling an uncut cigar between his fingers. He had no trouble picking the restaurant out; he'd grown proficient at spotting it from any of Kowloon's major business centres courtesy of his hours of distracted staring.

Even with his lawyer and partner here, he should have been attending. This deal was too important to insult with his inattention the very people he wanted to buy out. But the fact they were speaking in English instead of requiring him to negotiate in Mandarin meant they were already deferring. And that meant they had already decided to sell.

The rest was just a dance.

Meaning his attention was that much freer to wander across the harbour and up sixty storeys of steel.

His brain made him schedule a day full of Hong Kong meetings today, the twentieth, but his heart insisted they be here, in Kowloon, in full view of Qīngtíng across the harbour. As if he'd somehow know if a miracle occurred and Audrey turned up. As if his eyes would make her out, standing, arms folded around herself, against that wall of window. A distant speck against a sea of silver and chrome.

A point of business required him to refocus, but the moment it was addressed he let his gaze wander back to the restaurant, let his mind wander back to last Christmas. That extraordinary, dreamlike twenty-four hours.

He'd been as good as his word and never contacted Audrey again. No emails, no phone calls, no letters, no messages. Well, not the sort she'd warned him against, anyway. He always had a talent for loopholes.

But it had been purgatory this past year. What a fool he'd been to imagine he could just go back to his life in Shanghai and work her out of his system and get by on a steady diet of memories. He'd had to work at it—really freaking work—just to get through those first weeks. Then months. Then seasons.

And now the year had passed and the moment he'd dreaded was here.

The moment Audrey *didn't* come to Christmas.

Again.

She'd hit him with some home truths that day at the airport. Hard, overdue, unpleasant words that he'd promptly blocked out. It took him weeks to begin to digest them. First he'd used his anger to justify letting her leave. Then he rationalised and remembered how much pain she'd been in and how much courage it must have taken to stand there and let him have it with both barrels.

And finally he saw the sense of her words and, as if letting the words in made them material, he suddenly saw evidence of her truth everywhere he went. Getting in his face.

Mocking him.

His failure to form successful relationships *was* all about him. And he *had* used his friendship with Blake as a protective screen from behind which he indulged his feelings without having to own them.

And once the denial started to drop he saw more and more. How he'd lied to himself all this time believing it was his high standards that made it impossible for him to connect to just one woman. Hardly surprising he could never find her when that was the last thing his subconscious wanted.

He was no more honest with himself about why it didn't work out than he was with them.

But that was not the sort of epiphany a man could simply *un*see. So he began dating again, testing the theory, testing himself, hunting for someone who could offer him the same soul-connection that Audrey had offered that night in the chair. That she'd been offering him for years. Hungry to find what he'd had a taste of.

And it just wasn't there.

Even though—this time—he was genuinely open to finding it. And being unable to find someone as good as Audrey didn't get any more comfortable for being in the cold light of reason.

At least, before, he'd had all his denial to keep him company.

And so he'd thrown a lifebuoy out, courtesy of a favour someone owed him, and just hoped to heaven that Audrey was in a perceptive mood when the unsigned Christmas parcel was delivered last week. And receptive. Or even rabidly furious, as long as it was an emotion strong enough to bring her back to Hong Kong.

Back to the restaurant.

Back to him.

Because he had an apology to deliver. And a friendship to try and save. And possibly a fragile, wounded spirit to save, too.

Behind him, the massive boardroom doors snicked softly and opened. Jeannie Ling murmured in the ear of the man closest to the door and he nodded then tapped a few keys into his tablet surreptitiously.

Seconds later Oliver's smartphone vibrated.

He glanced down disinterestedly at the subject line of his partner's email:

*Ph. Msg-urgent*

But then his body was up and out of his chair even before his mind had fully registered the words and phone number on the next line, and he was halfway to the door before any of the ridiculously wealthy and overly entitled people in the room realised what was happening.

*Pls call Ming-húa*

*He hadn't come.*

Audrey stared into the busy, oblivious world of Qīngtíng's dragonflies and cursed herself for the ideological fool she was.

Of course he hadn't come. He'd moved on. The online gossip sheets made that patently clear. In fact he'd probably moved on by last Christmas. Whatever they'd shared here in Hong Kong was ancient history. Solstice fever. Even the restaurant had gone back to being what it was. Just a place you went to eat food.

She glanced over towards the restaurant's festively decorated glass wall. The smoking chair was no longer resident.

*Their* chair.

Hastily removed as a bad memory, probably. Or quite possibly a hygiene issue.

Heat flooded her cheeks but the dragonflies didn't much care. They went about their business, zipping around, feeding and frolicking and dipping their many feet in the crystalline water that circulated through their beautiful, make-believe world. Only a single individual battered against the corner of the terrarium, repeatedly. Uselessly.

She knew exactly how it felt.

Most of what she'd done this past year was useless battering. Existing, but not really living. Punctuated by insane bouts of emotional self-harm whenever her discipline failed her and she'd do the whole stalker number online and search out any clues about Oliver.

What he was up to. *Who* he was up to. Whether he was okay.

Of course, he always was.

On her weak days, she imagined that Oliver never contacting her again was him honouring her request, respecting her, and she'd get all sore and squishy inside and struggle with the reality that it was over. But on her stronger days she'd accept the reality—that not contacting her was probably a blessed relief for a man like The Hammer and that there was nothing to really *be* over.

Nothing had even started.

If you didn't count the wild sex.

She'd vacillate between bouts of self-judgement for her stupidity, and fierce self-defence that she'd fallen for a man like him, convincing herself that it was possible for someone to be a pretty good *guy* without necessarily managing to always be a good *person*.

Except that, like it or not, he'd been more than pretty good. Oliver was exceptional. In so many ways. And knowing that only made his inability to love her all the more brutal.

What the hell was she thinking coming here? She could have done what she needed to do by email.

Almost as she had the thought, a flurry of low voices drew her focus, through the terrarium, past the dragonflies, over to the restaurant's glamorous entrance.

To the man who'd just burst in.

*Oliver.*

Her whole body locked up and she mentally scrabbled around for somewhere to hide. Under her sofa. In the lush terrarium planting with the dragonflies. Anywhere other than here, with the terrified-bunny look on her face, peering at him through the glass like the coward she wanted so badly not to be.

It took his laser-focus only a heartbeat to find her.

His legs started moving. His eyes remained locked on hers as he powered around the outside of the terrarium and stopped just a metre away. His intent gaze whispered her name even though no air crossed his lips.

'Explain,' she gasped aloud, before she did something more ill-advised.

Not, *'Hello Oliver,'* not, *'How dare you look so good after such a crap year?'*; not even, *'Why are you here?'* All much more pressing issues.

'Explain what?' he said, infuriating in his calmness. As if this weren't the biggest deal ever.

'Why my Testore trail leads to you.'

His steady eyes didn't waver. 'Does it?'

'Why the instrument I've been slowly working my way towards for two years suddenly turns up in a luggage locker at Hongqiao train station.'

He stepped one pace closer. 'Asia's biggest train station. I imagine that's not the only secret it's harbouring.'

Both arms folded across her chest. 'Shanghai, Oliver.'

'Coincidence.'

'What did you do?' Every word a bullet.

He studied the dragonflies for distracted moments and when he brought his eyes back to hers they were defiant. 'I made a few phone calls. Called in a few favours.' He shrugged. 'It's not like I donated a kidney.'

She peered at him through narrowed eyes. 'You just happened to be owed a favour by the exact someone who knew where the Testore was?'

He sized her up, as if trying to determine how far he could take the nonchalance. 'Look…I called in a marker with a colleague, they called one in from someone else and it reverse dominoed all the way up to someone who knew the right people to ask.'

'And then what?'

'Then I bought it.'

'A million-dollar instrument?'

'Can you put a price on a trafficked child?'

*Ha ha.* 'You realise you're an accessory to a crime, now?'

His eyes grew uncertain for the first time since he'd walked in the door and he frowned. 'I hoped I'd get bonus points for repatriating it.'

But she wasn't ready to give him those points yet. 'You perpetuated the problem by rewarding the syndicate for their crime. Now they'll go out and steal another cello.'

'Is that really what's bothering you, Audrey? Wasn't it more important to get the cello back into safe hands than to arrest whatever mid-level thug with a drug-debt they'd have made take the fall?'

*Did* it matter how the Testore was recovered or what favours were exchanged and promises made? Or did it only matter that its rightful owner literally broke down and sobbed when it was returned to her, triggering Audrey's own tears—tears she'd thought she'd used completely up?

Maybe it only mattered that Oliver had cared enough to try.

'What's bothering me is why you did it.' And by 'bother' she meant 'making my chest ache'.

'Because I could.' He shrugged. 'I have connections that you would never have had access to.'

'A million dollars, Oliver.' Plus some change. 'Excessive, even for you.'

'Not if it helped you out.'

Blinking didn't make the words any easier to comprehend—or believe—but this was not the time to let subtext get the better of her. 'I'm amazed that you have any fortune at all if you make such emotionally based decisions.'

'I don't, generally. Only with you.'

'Did you think I wouldn't figure it out?' That an anonymous key in a Christmas parcel leading her to a Shanghai train station wouldn't be clue enough?

'I knew you would.'

'So did you think I'd gush with gratitude?'

'On the contrary. I hoped it might piss you off enough to get on a plane.'

Manipulated again. By the master. She shook her head. 'Well, here I am. Hope you don't want your million bucks back.'

'Forget the money, Audrey. I sold one of my company's nine executive apartments to raise the cash. It had only been used twice last year.'

The world he lived in.

'What if I'd just taken the cello and run?'

That resulted in insta-frown. 'Then I'd have been no worse off.'

Ugh. 'This was a mistake.'

'Audrey—' his voice suspended her flight after only two steps '—wait.'

She ignored his command. 'Thank you for doing my job for me. I'll put a good word in with the authorities for you.'

'You're leaving?'

'Yes. I shouldn't have come at all.'

What she should do was get back onto her ridiculously expensive short-notice flight and head back to her ridiculously expensive Sydney house. Blake's house that she'd not had the courage or energy to move out of. The house and the life she hated.

He stepped round in front of her. 'Why did you?'

Because she was slowly dying inside knowing she'd never see him again? Because she'd managed the first six months on pride and adrenaline but now there was nothing left but sorrow. Because she was addicted.

'No idea,' she gritted. 'Let me rectify that right now.'

He sprinted in front of her again. 'Audrey, wait, please just hear me out.'

'Didn't we say enough at the airport?' she sighed.

'You said quite a lot but I was pretty much speechless.'

Seriously? He got her back here to have the last word?

'Ten minutes, Audrey. That's it.'

It was impossible to be this close to those bottomless hazel eyes and not give him what he was asking. Ten minutes of her time. In return for a million-dollar cello.

She crossed her arms and settled into the carpet more firmly. 'Fine. Clock's ticking.'

'Not here,' he said, sliding his hand to her lower back and directing her towards the door.

She stopped and lurched free of his hot touch. 'No. Not upstairs.' That had way too many memories. Although, reasonably, there were just as many down here.

But at least, here, there was an audience. Chaperones.

*What are you afraid of?* he'd once challenged her. *Me or yourself?*

He just stared, a stoic plea in his eyes.

'Oh, for God's sake, fine!' She swivelled ahead of him and marched back out into the elevator lobby then up the circular stairs off to the side. The plush carpet disguised his footfalls but she could feel Oliver's closeness, his eyes on her behind.

'You've lost weight,' he announced.

She froze. Turned. Glared.

Yes, she'd bloody well lost weight and she really didn't have much to spare. Now her 'athletic' was more 'catwalk' than she'd have liked. Especially for preservation of dignity. She didn't want him knowing how tough she'd been doing it.

His hands immediately shot up either side of him. 'Right, sorry…keep going. Ten minutes.'

At the top, he passed her and ran his key card through the swipe and the big doors swung open just as they had last year. She followed him into the luxurious penthouse—

—and stopped dead just a few feet in, all the fight sucking clear out of her.

Over by the window, over where he'd first touched her with trembling hands all those long, lonely nights ago, a new piece of furniture had pride of place overlooking the view.

An overstuffed smoking chair.

*Their* chair.

The sight numbed her—emotionally and literally.

'Why is that here?' she whispered.

He seemed surprised by the direction of her gaze. 'I had it brought up here. I like to sit on it, look out. Think.'

'About what?'

'A lot of things.' He took a breath. 'Us, mostly.'

She turned wide eyes on him 'There is no "us".'

His shoulders sagged. 'There was. For one amazing night. I think about that, and I miss it.'

Every muscle fibre in her body tightened up, ready for the 'but'.

He stepped closer. 'I sit in that chair and I think about you and I miss *you.*'

'Careful,' she squeezed out of an airless chest. 'I might get the wrong idea and let my *feelings* get away with me.'

When had she become so angry?

He took her hand, seemed surprised by its frigidity, and led her to the luxurious sofa circling the raised floor of the formal area. The sofa that they'd made such fast, furious love on that first time. She pulled her fingers free and crossed to the chair, instead, curling her hands around its ornate back, borrowing its strength. Using it as a crutch.

Exactly the way her memories of it had been this past year.

'I need you to know something,' he said. 'Quite a few somethings, actually.'

She straightened, listening, but didn't turn around. The Hong Kong skyline soothed her. Speaking of things missed…

'I started wanting you about ten minutes after you walked into that bar all those years ago.' The greenish-brown of his eyes focused in hard. 'Then in the years that followed, I would have given every cent I had to wake up to you just once instead of clock-watching as midnight approached and waiting for the moment you'd flee down the stairs until the following Christmas.'

Her breath slammed up behind the fist his words caused in her chest until she remembered that 'wanting' was not the same as *'wanting'*.

One was short-term and easily addressed, apparently. Maybe that was why he'd lured her back here. Round two.

'I was captivated from the first time you locked those expressive eyes and that sharp mind on me. You were a challenge because you seemed so disinterested in me and so interested in Blake and that just didn't happen to me. And I'd sit there, enduring Blake's hands all over you—'

'Embarrassed by it.'

'Not embarrassed, Audrey. Pained. I hated watching him touch you. I hated thinking you preferred his company, his touch, to mine. And that was when I realised there was more than just ego going on. That I didn't just *want* you. I had *feelings* for you.'

Her fingers curled into the brocade chair-back and she whispered, 'Why did you send me the key, Oliver?'

'Because you were right and because I wanted to tell you that, face to face, and I thought it would get your attention.'

'Right about what?'

'All of it. The Heathcliff thing. It was so much easier to
be consumed with longing and never have to face the reality of what that actually meant. And then to disguise that
with work and endless other excuses. You were my best
friend's wife. As unattainable as any woman could possibly be. Completely safe to fixate on.

'I convinced myself that my inability to connect to
women—just one woman—was about having high standards. It was easy to find them wanting and easier still to
disregard them because they failed to measure up to this
totally unattainable idyll I had. The idea of you.'

He came around in front of the chair, folded one knee
on its thick cushion to level their heights and met her eyes.
'I would find fault with the relationships before they got
anywhere near the point of commitment purely to avoid
having to face that moment.'

The anguish in his face wheedled its way under her skin
and she itched to touch him. But discipline, for once, did
not fail her. 'Which moment?'

'The moment where I realised that I wasn't actually capable of committing to them. That I was no more capable
of being true to someone than my father. So I'd get out before I had to face that or I chose women who would cheat
on me first.'

*Oh, Oliver...*

'I counted myself so superior to him all this time—me
with my rigid values and my high moral ground—but the
whole time I was terrified that I had inherited his inability
to commit to someone. To love just one someone.' He lifted
harrowed eyes to hers. 'And that if ever I let myself, then
I'd be exposed as my father's son to someone to whom it
would really matter.'

He stroked her cheek.

'But then I had you. In my arms. In my bed. And every
single thing I'd ever wanted was being handed to me on a

platter. The woman against whom every other woman I'd ever met had paled. It was all so suddenly *real*, and there was no good reason for us not to be together—in this chair, in this room, in this town and beyond it. I panicked.'

'You told me you couldn't see yourself loving me. You were quite clear.' Saying it aloud still hurt, even after all this time.

'Audrey.' He sighed. 'My father took my mother's love for him and used it to bind her in a relationship that he didn't have to work for. He didn't value it. He certainly didn't honour it. What if I did that to you?'

'What if you didn't? You aren't your father, Oliver.' No matter what she'd said in anger.

'What if I am?' Desperation clouded his eyes. 'Your feelings were going to force me into discovering. That's why I pushed you away.'

Just twelve months ago she'd stood here, in this penthouse, terrified that she was somehow deficient. And Oliver had proven her wrong. And in doing so changed her life. Now was her chance to return the favour.

'You are not broken, Oliver Harmer. And you are as much your mother's son as you are your father's. Never forget that.'

He suddenly found something in the giant Christmas tree in the corner enormously fascinating, as if he couldn't quite believe her words were true.

'Could she love?' Audrey pressed.

'Yes.'

'Then why can't you?'

Confusion mixed in with the anguish. 'I never have.'

'Have you not? Truly?' She straightened and locked her eyes. 'Can you think of no one at all?'

He stood frozen.

She kept her courage. 'It can be easy to overlook. I once loved someone for eight years, almost without realising.'

His skin blanched and it was hard to know whether it was because she'd used the L word in connection with him or because she'd used the past tense.

'When did you realise?'

She ran her hands across the back of the chair's fine embroidered fabric. 'Out of the blue, this one time, curled up in a chair.'

He still just stared. Silence ticked on. She forced herself to remain tough.

'So, was that what you wanted to tell me?' she checked. *'It's not you it's me?'*

'It *is* me, Audrey. But no, what I really wanted to do was apologise. I'm sorry I let you leave Hong Kong believing there was anything you could have done differently or anything you could have been that would have made a difference.'

And his guilt was apparently worth a rare cello.

Her lips tightened. 'You know, this seems to be the story of my life. Last time it was my gender, this time there was nothing I could have done differently short of *caring less*.'

'This is nothing like Blake.'

'I'm not ashamed of my feelings. And I'm not afraid of them either. Unlike you.'

His eyes tarnished off as she watched. 'Meaning?'

'Exactly what I said. I think you are afraid of the depth of your feelings. Because feeling makes you vulnerable.'

'What I'm afraid of is hurting you.'

'Isn't that my risk to take? Just as it was your mother's choice to stay with your father.'

Two deep lines cut down between his brows. 'You can't *want* to make that choice.'

'I wouldn't if I believed that you've inherited anything more than eye colour from your father. You dislike him too much. If anything I'd expect you to grow into the complete opposite of him just out of sheer bloody determination.'

'I saw what losing his love did to my mother.' Tense and tight but not angry. 'How vulnerable it made her.'

'Don't you trust me?'

'You know I do.'

'Then why do you think I would hurt you?' she begged. 'I chose to be vulnerable with you last Christmas because I couldn't think of a single person in the world that I trusted more with my unshielded heart.'

'I'm afraid I might hurt *you*.'

'By possibly abandoning me at some point in the future?'

'I saw what it did to my mother.' For the first time, the tension in his face hinted at hostility. Except, now, she knew that was what fear looked like on him. 'And I felt what it did to me.'

She sucked in a breath, loud and punctuated in the frozen moments of silence before he crossed to the edge of the sofa. He pulled a hanging tinsel ball into his hands and punished it with attention.

'You?' she risked.

He spun. 'My father opted out of his *family*, Audrey, not just his marriage. He abandoned me, too.'

'But he didn't abandon you. He's still there now.'

Bleak eyes stared out of the window. 'Yeah, he did. He just couldn't be arsed leaving.'

For a heartbeat, Audrey wondered if she'd pushed him too far, but then that big body slumped down onto the sofa, head bowed.

She crossed to his side, sat next to him, curled her hand over his and said the only thing she could think of. 'I'm sorry.'

He shook his head.

She turned more into him. 'I'm sorry that it happened. And I'm sorry that it has affected you all this time. Love is not supposed to work that way.'

As her arms came up he tipped down into them, into

her hold and slid his own around her middle. She embraced him with everything she had in her. This was Oliver after all, the man she loved.

And the man she loved was hurting.

He buried his face in her neck and she rocked him, gently. One big hand slid up into her hair, keeping her close, and she felt the damp of tears against her neck.

'You can love, Oliver,' she said, after minutes of silent embrace. 'I promise. You just need to let yourself. And trust that it's safe to do it with me.'

His silence reeked of doubt.

She stroked his hair back. 'Maybe your love is just like one of the companies you rescue. Broken down by someone who didn't value it and treat it right. So maybe you just need to get it into the hands of someone who will nurture and protect it. And grow it to its full potential. Because you have so much potential. And so do we.'

His half-smile, when he sat up straighter, told her exactly how lame that analogy was. But too bad, she was committed to it now.

'Someone like who?'

'Someone like me. I'm looking to diversify my portfolio, as it happens.'

'Really?'

She shrugged. 'I had a bad investment myself not so long ago, something that could have been very different if I'd given it the time and focus it deserved. But I've learned from my mistakes and know what to do differently next time.'

His smile twisted. 'Well, no one's perfect.'

'So how about it? Think I might be the sort of person you'd trust a damaged company to? I come highly recommended for my work in the recovery of trafficked stringed instruments.'

He nodded and pressed a grateful kiss to her forehead. 'Very responsible. And honourable.'

'And I have federal security clearance,' she breathed as he pressed another one to her jaw. 'They don't give those to just anyone. At all.'

His nod was serious. 'Hard to argue with Interpol.'

'And…um…' She lost her train of thought as his lips found the hollow between her collarbones. 'I have a blue library card. It means I can take books out of the reference section.'

Kiss. 'Persuasive.'

'And I'm not *him* any more than you are.' The lips stopped dead, pressed into her shoulder. 'So if I'm willing to take a risk on you despite the fact you've already hurt me once, the least you can do is return the favour.'

He pulled away to stare into her eyes for the longest time.

Then, in the space between breaths, the cool damp of his butterfly kisses became the warm damp of his mouth working its way up her throat. Her jaw. Roaming. Exploring. Rediscovering.

'I never should have let you go,' he breathed, hot against her ear, right before tonguing her lobe.

She twisted into him, seeking his lips. 'You had to. So I could come back to you, again.'

And then they were kissing. Hot and hard and frantic. Slow and deep and healing.

'I don't want to love anyone else,' he grated, twisting her under him and pressing her into the sofa with his strength. 'I don't want to trust anyone else. Only you, Audrey. It was only ever you.'

He stroked her hair back and applied kiss after kiss to her eyelids, cheekbones, forehead. Worshipping with his mouth. She reached up and stilled his hands, stilled his lips with her own and caught his eyes and held them.

'I love you, Oliver. I always have. I always will. And

my love makes me stronger and better whether we're together or not.'

He twisted so that they faced each other on the spacious
couch. 'I don't ever want to go hours without you, let alone
months. Not again.'

'Then that's how we'll do it,' she breathed. 'One day at
a time. Until days have become weeks and weeks years,
and before you know it we'll have been together, in love,
as long as we were apart, in love.'

'I can't imagine what it would have been like being alone
without loving you all those years. How desolate it would
have been.'

*Loving you...*

There was such veracity in the way it just slipped out in
the middle of that sentence. As though it had always been
a part of his subconscious and they weren't the most important words she'd ever heard.

Her laugh was five-eighths sob.

Something occurred to him then. 'Imagine if we'd never
met. If you'd gone to the bar next door that day. I wouldn't
have had you to keep me sane all this time.'

'Imagine if I'd been braver that first day and actually
managed a proper conversation with you.'

'I never would have let you go,' he vowed.

'We'd be an old married couple by now.'

His smile bit into her ear. 'We'd be the horniest married
couple Hong Kong had ever seen.'

She lifted her head. 'Hong Kong?'

'We'd have lived here, wouldn't we?'

Audrey considered that. 'Yeah, I think we would. Maybe
you would have bought this penthouse anyway.'

'I bought the restaurant for you, after you didn't come,
so I would always have you.'

'A little excessive, really.'

He huffed. 'A little desperate.'

She traced his lip with her tongue tip. 'I love you, desperate.'

'I love you, period.'

Okay, so she didn't mind hearing it formally, too. She would never, ever tire of hearing it.

They studied each other, drowning in each other's depths and tangling their fingers.

'I have a gift for you,' he said almost sheepishly as he crossed to the expensive tree in the corner.

'The cello wasn't enough?'

He handed her the parcel, small and suspiciously square and faultlessly gift-wrapped. 'I would have sent it to you if you hadn't come.'

'The paper is too perfect to ruin—'

He took the parcel from her and tore the beautiful bow off the top, then handed it back. Problem solved.

Inside a distinctive jeweller's box taunted her. 'Oliver...'

'Don't panic. It's not a ring,' he assured. 'Not this time.'

*Not this time...*

A tiny leather tie lifted off the clasp and let her open the box. She couldn't help the soft gasp. Inside, resting as though it had just alighted on the black silk pillow, was an exquisite stylised dragonfly necklace, its tiny white-gold body encrusted with gemstones and its fine wings a mix of aquamarine and laser-cut sapphire. At its head, a woman's torso carved from jade, bare-breasted and beautiful.

'That reminded me of you,' he murmured, almost apologetic. 'Wild and stylish and natural all at once. I had to have it.'

Tears welled so violently it was almost impossible to appreciate the handcrafted beauty. 'It's...'

Were there enough words to sum up what this meant to her? Such a personal and special gift. More meaningful than any cello. Or restaurant. Or penthouse.

This was up there with the chair for things she'd run

back into a burning high-rise for. She pressed herself into his arms, the jeweller's box curled into one of the fists she snaked around his neck.

'It's perfect,' she breathed against his ear. 'Thank you.'

Her teary kiss was more eloquent than she could ever be and so she buried herself in his chest, crawling onto the sofa with him and letting the thrum of her heartbeat against his communicate for her. He draped the dragonfly around her neck and it nestled down between her breasts. Over her heart.

Oliver busied himself playing with it, alternating between stroking it and the breasts either side of it. Slowly the dragonfly heated with the warmth coming off her.

'Do you think Blake sensed it?' she said, after some time, to distract herself from his talented fingers. 'How drawn to each other we were?'

'What makes you ask that?'

'He was always so uptight when I was around you. I figured maybe he could sense my attraction.'

'Are you kidding? You have the best poker face in the world. I had no clue and I was perpetually on alert for the slightest sign.' She frowned and he kissed it away. 'I think it's more likely he could sense my attraction. I'm a mere grasshopper to your sensei of emotional discipline.'

'But why would he care if you were attracted to me, given what we now know?'

'Dog in a manger?' Oliver nibbled his way up her shoulder blades. 'Maybe he resented my attention to his property.'

As tempting as it was to drop the conversation and find out where all that nibbling would lead to, something in her just wouldn't let it go. 'It wasn't resentment. It was envy.'

He grinned and it just needed an unlit cigar to be perfect. 'Maybe it wasn't about you? I *am* pretty sexy…'

He laughed but Audrey sat up on her elbow, considered him. 'And Blake *was* pretty gay.'

'No, Audrey. I was kidding.'

Her whole body tingled with revelation. 'He was jealous *for* you, not *of* you. That makes so much more sense.'

Something final clicked into place. How flustered Blake used to get if she came to dinner looking hot. It wasn't attraction, it was anger—that Oliver might grow interested. And all the random, unprovoked touching…that must have been designed to get a reaction out of Oliver, not her.

Maybe Blake had loved his best friend for more years than she had.

'He wanted you,' she said. 'And you wanted me. And he saw that every single time we were all together.'

There was a weird kind of certainty in the thought. No wonder he thought there was something going on in Hong Kong. He knew the truth. He just knew it much earlier than either of them.

'Poor Blake,' she whispered. 'Trapped behind so many masks. And you and I were supposed to be together all along.'

There was just no question. Again, that strange cosmic rightness.

'We may be slow,' he said, burrowing into the place below her ear, 'but we got there.'

'Promise me no masks between us, Oliver. Ever. Promise me we'll go back to Audrey and Oliver who can talk about anything, who will share anything. Even the tough stuff.'

He kissed his way to her lips, then, seeing how very serious she was about that, he rested his chin on her forehead and placed his hand on her heart. 'I give you my solemn oath, Audrey. Whenever we have something tough to discuss we'll curl up in that chair and talk it out and we won't leave it until we're done. No matter what.'

Her eyes shifted right. 'Our chair?'

'Our chair.' He lifted his chin to stare into her eyes. 'Why?'

'I was hoping it could be used more for evil than for good,' she breathed. 'And it has been a very, very long time between chairs.'

Desire flooded Oliver's gorgeous gaze. 'Fortunately, it's a multipurpose chair. But, come on.' He pulled her to her feet and towards the window. 'Let's make sure it's *fit* for purpose.'

\* \* \* \* \*

# ROMANCE

| | |
|---|---|
| **Million Dollar Christmas Proposal** | Lucy Monroe |
| **A Dangerous Solace** | Lucy Ellis |
| **The Consequences of That Night** | Jennie Lucas |
| **Secrets of a Powerful Man** | Chantelle Shaw |
| **Never Gamble with a Caffarelli** | Melanie Milburne |
| **Visconti's Forgotten Heir** | Elizabeth Power |
| **A Touch of Temptation** | Tara Pammi |
| **A Scandal in the Headlines** | Caitlin Crews |
| **What the Bride Didn't Know** | Kelly Hunter |
| **Mistletoe Not Required** | Anne Oliver |
| **Proposal at the Lazy S Ranch** | Patricia Thayer |
| **A Little Bit of Holiday Magic** | Melissa McClone |
| **A Cadence Creek Christmas** | Donna Alward |
| **Marry Me under the Mistletoe** | Rebecca Winters |
| **His Until Midnight** | Nikki Logan |
| **The One She Was Warned About** | Shoma Narayanan |
| **Her Firefighter Under the Mistletoe** | Scarlet Wilson |
| **Christmas Eve Delivery** | Connie Cox |

# MEDICAL

| | |
|---|---|
| **Gold Coast Angels: Bundle of Trouble** | Fiona Lowe |
| **Gold Coast Angels: How to Resist Temptation** | Amy Andrews |
| **Snowbound with Dr Delectable** | Susan Carlisle |
| **Her Real Family Christmas** | Kate Hardy |

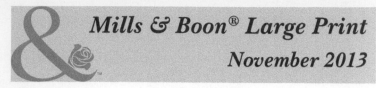

# Mills & Boon® Large Print
## November 2013

# ROMANCE

| | |
|---|---|
| **His Most Exquisite Conquest** | Emma Darcy |
| **One Night Heir** | Lucy Monroe |
| **His Brand of Passion** | Kate Hewitt |
| **The Return of Her Past** | Lindsay Armstrong |
| **The Couple who Fooled the World** | Maisey Yates |
| **Proof of Their Sin** | Dani Collins |
| **In Petrakis's Power** | Maggie Cox |
| **A Cowboy To Come Home To** | Donna Alward |
| **How to Melt a Frozen Heart** | Cara Colter |
| **The Cattleman's Ready-Made Family** | Michelle Douglas |
| **What the Paparazzi Didn't See** | Nicola Marsh |

# HISTORICAL

| | |
|---|---|
| **Mistress to the Marquis** | Margaret McPhee |
| **A Lady Risks All** | Bronwyn Scott |
| **Her Highland Protector** | Ann Lethbridge |
| **Lady Isobel's Champion** | Carol Townend |
| **No Role for a Gentleman** | Gail Whitiker |

# MEDICAL

| | |
|---|---|
| **NYC Angels: Flirting with Danger** | Tina Beckett |
| **NYC Angels: Tempting Nurse Scarlet** | Wendy S. Marcus |
| **One Life Changing Moment** | Lucy Clark |
| **P.S. You're a Daddy!** | Dianne Drake |
| **Return of the Rebel Doctor** | Joanna Neil |
| **One Baby Step at a Time** | Meredith Webber |